T0169667

Good Night, Mr. Kissinger

and other stories

Good Night, Mr. Kissinger

and other stories

K. Anis Ahmed

Unnamed Press
Los Angeles, CA

Unnamed Press
Los Angeles
www.unnamedpress.com

This book is a work of fiction. Names, characters, places and incidents
are wholly fictional or are used fictitiously. Any resemblance to actual events
or persons, living or dead, is entirely coincidental.

"Good Night, Mr. Kissinger"
Copyright © K. Anis Ahmed
This book was first published in 2012 in Bangladesh by
the University Press Limited.
All rights reserved, including the right to reproduce this book or
portions thereof in any form whatsoever.
ISBN 978-1-939419-04-0

To Juditha

Acknowledgments

This work was made possible by the encouragement of many individuals to whom I feel deeply indebted. First, the two editors who published most of these stories in local magazines or anthologies in Dhaka—Niaz Zaman and Khademul Islam. For moral support I thank Writer's Bloc for their great generosity towards me, in particular: Shazia Omar, Sadaf Saaz Siddiqui, Farah Guzhnavi and Awrup Sanyal. Fellow writers who provided steady inspiration through the years: Matt Leibel, Chris Heiser (now my American publisher at Unnamed Press), Jeffrey Yang, Maria Chaudhuri, and the old culprits Hozy Rossi and Neal Durando. The book has been improved a great deal by feedback from Professor Kaiser Haq. I also thank Shashi Tharoor and Tahmima Anam for their valuable inputs. The final copy would never be what it is without the amazing editorial intervention by Michelle Alumkal (any faults still remaining are, sadly, entirely mine). Mahrukh Mohiuddin, my first publisher at the University Press Limited, in Bangladesh, was full of genuine warmth for her writers. I will always be grateful for her acceptance of *Good Night, Mr. Kissinger.* Many other friends and mentors have left an indelible mark on my evolution as a writer: teachers Stanley Elkin and Edmund White; and friends Joy Katz, Kylie Jill, Sanjit Basu and Melissa Myambo. I have been supremely lucky to have a family that supported my writing: my parents Kazi Shahid Ahmed and Ameenah Ahmed, for never telling me what I had to be in life; my brother Inam, for his unwavering enthusiasm; and primarily my brother Nabil, for believing first and always. But above all, my one guiding light who makes it all possible, is my wife, Juditha, and this book is dedicated to her.

K. Anis Ahmed
Dhaka, January 2014

Table of Contents

Chameli

The house at the very end of the street, heavily encircled by trees, over-looking one of the darkest and wider parts of the lake, sat unfinished for a year. In the autumn of 1970, however, a few men showed up with ladders and toolkits and went vigorously to work. Sloppily they applied a pale blue color on the one-story building. A purblind gardener, who tended to a few other houses on the street, pulled out weeds and other wild vegetation from the tiny front yard.

None of the boys who lived on that street, except Galib, registered these changes. However, it wasn't the house but the new neighbors that grabbed his attention. First he noticed only the father: a giant of a man, who lumbered with his gaze set on things far off in the distance. Then the next day, as he was about to open his gate on the way back from a football match, some whisper of instinct made him turn, and across the dusk-descendant street he captured the elements of an apparition—blue dress, white skin, a long, swinging pony-tail—disappearing into the little blue house. For only a second he glimpsed these signs and in that second they robbed him of all peace, demanding relentlessly that the picture be completed.

Until the moment of that first sighting Galib was a boy like any other on the street. He was fanatical about football, and left behind a trail of hobbies—toy cars, kites, lackadaisical stamp and coin collections. In a fit of individualism, he had also spent a futile season, coached by

the gardener, mastering various bird-calls that were supposed to make
the creatures alight on nearby trees. He disliked homework, being force-
fed fruits and vitamins, and more strongly he resented more strongly
the contradictory and dictatorial nature of adults. He also suffered from
an incipient and prurient interest in the female form. Above all else,
though, he was carefree; but he did not know nearly enough yet to appreciate the rarity of that joy.

From the moment he saw the girl he was forced into a double life.
One in which he struggled to abide by his old obligations, and his real
life, which now centered on mute obsession with her. It took a few days
before he could get a chance to see her again. He discovered that she
came out of her gate at exactly seven and, though it was a bit early for his
school time, so did Galib.

By now Galib had found out from the gardener that the girl had no
mother, that they were Punjabis, and that her name was Chameli. An
unusual name for a Punjabi, he thought, but he did not really think of
her as a Punjabi at that time. Every morning father and daughter came
out together. The father in a starched white shirt and a thin tie, and the
girl in her school-dress. She'd find some pretext—to fix her hair or her
school-dress or to point at something—to disengage her small white hand
from her father's enormous grip the moment she spotted Galib. This secret sign allowed his twelve-year-old heart to pass one more day in hope.

Two weeks later Galib twisted his ankle, trying to jump off the top of
the school stairs. At first he was deeply annoyed, but soon he realized the
benefits of this apparent setback: he was no longer obliged to go to practice every afternoon. Rather, once he was fit enough to limp outside, he
would travel out to the no-man's land between his and Chameli's gates,
or wander off to the lake-side. They had made eye contact by now, but
he didn't know how to approach her. It wasn't like he had never spoken
to a girl before. Admittedly, he had not had much practice; he went to
an all-boys' school. Still, there were birthday parties and the weddings.
And there was his best friend Tabu's sister, who lived at the other end of

the same street. Being gap-toothed and strident, however, she held little interest for him and their talks were limited to Tabu's whereabouts.

Every afternoon he stepped out rehearsing possible scenes of encounter in his mind. As the minutes fell away the possibilities shrank. Some days Chameli did not come out of her house at all. Other days she came out on her bike and sped off in the other direction. Even though she did not shy away from meeting his eyes, she offered no further gestures of support. Every time he saw her, the world receded into blackness, and she bloomed like a lone star in this private firmament. He didn't know how to talk to someone who defied ordinary matrices of apprehension. Forlorn, he spent the vanishing crumbs of each daylight skipping stones on the lake surface.

Once his ankle recovered, he still feigned mild pains to avoid practice. One of these days they'd make contact! Till then, however, he had to while away the hours of vigil somewhere. And he chose to do so with the gardener. At that hour, the man could often be found slumped against the wall of one of the many gardens under his care. His customary white skull-cap and foggy glasses doffed, he'd be in peaceful siesta until Galib rudely awakened him. The man had an infinite tolerance for life's intrusions, and once awoken he'd calmly set about rolling a bidi. With great deliberation he'd explain to Galib the perfect method: it was not just a matter of leaf or twisting, but like gardening, it required patience and devotion. Once the perfect bidi was rolled, he'd allow Galib to take a few puffs, and sometimes to smoke away an entire stick.

In the middle of these bidi-rolling sessions one day, when they'd chosen the outer wall of Galib's house as their perch, Chameli came out to the water-side. She had not noticed them, and desultorily she picked up a rock to throw at the water. The gardener gently took the bidi out of Galib's hands, fearful perhaps that the young man might mangle it in his distraction. Galib walked up tremulously to where Chameli stood and stopped just a few steps behind her. Not only did she have imperfect technique, but even her choice of the stones was faulty. Galib watched Chameli chuck several stones that plopped feebly on the water surface once or twice before going under. He walked up to her with a perfect throwing specimen, with just the right curvature and weight, and said, "Try this one. And try to chuck it more with your wrist than with your arm."

Chameli took the piece of pottery without looking at him. She studied the water intently, while he studied her with equal intensity. He had never stood this close to her, and he felt intoxicated by a strong fragrance of powder or soap, or who knew what alchemy women used—even at her age—to make themselves so much pleasanter to look at or smell. Chameli took a step back and then two forward, sending the grey shard with a jerk of the wrist to four clean skips on the surface of the water. She jumped around with great glee and said, "It worked! You were right! It worked!"

By now he had already picked out another choice projectile to continue Chameli's training. Every afternoon, for the next few days, they met by the lake-side, while Galib coached Chameli: the wind-up, the twisting of the hips, the seamless flow of speed and motion from hip to shoulders, and shoulders to wrist. After a week, without premeditation, he touched her arm to show what might be the perfect angle of release. That night his inflamed mind refused to go to sleep. The touch of her skin, the rhythm of her breath, still audible in his heart, provoked sensations that he could neither suppress nor satisfy. He had already given her a place of pure adoration in his heart with which such urges were incongruous, dishonorable. How his body revolted against all that was good in his soul!

The next day, as he was about to leave his gates, he was confronted by Tabu, who stood there with his boots slung over his shoulders, chewing gum. "So, when are you coming back to practice?"

"I don't know. When the doctor says," answered Galib grimly.

"Your foot should be fine by now," said Tabu. "We don't have a striker, the match is next week."

"It's not my foot; it's my ankle, you dumb-bell. And what do you know when it should be fine? You're a doctor now?"

"Nope, but I see you chucking stones by the lake every day," said Tabu with a mischievous grin. Never before had Galib noticed how ugly his friend looked. He was short and chubby, sported dirty, curly hair, and stank like a pig. Other violent thoughts about Tabu, and all the other boys on his team, seized his mind. But, he controlled himself, and replied, "Why don't you mind your own business?"

"Because your business is so much prettier," said Tabu, and jumped back from the gate which Galib swung out with force to strike his friend. "May be I'll tell the other boys, may be we'll all come and chuck stones."

Galib suddenly felt his eyes stinging and his voice choked. He could not possibly explain to Tabu what he felt for Chameli. All his friends were still innocents, philistines, animals. They were incapable of understanding anything sacred. He did not want Chameli's name besmirched in a conversation with the likes of Tabu, but showing any further emotion on this topic would only make matters worse. Even in this state of lonely indignation, he stayed clear enough to recognize that. Barely able to conceal the quaver in his voice, he said, "I'll come from next week maybe."

Tabu was already walking away from him, and shouted over his shoulder, "See you next week, stone-chucker."

Tabu was not the only one who seemed to have divined his secret. Galib's mother had asked him about the girl across the street. She had asked if he didn't want to invite her over one day for tea. *No, I don't! I don't want any of you to meet her! I want a world where only she and I exist.* He wanted no one else in that world. Not his mother, not her father, not Tabu, nor any other being who might threaten the delicate, dulcet tone of their belonging.

The gardener was his only ally in this anguishing pursuit. With great impassivity, he would give Galib relevant updates: "Chameli mem won't be coming out today; father's very angry with her," "Chameli mem broke her pen today, she's very upset," "Chameli mem asked where you've been the last two days."

But what about Chameli herself? Did she know how he felt about her? Did she have any inkling of the ridiculous fantasies he wove involving the two of them far into the fathomless future? Did she feel the same way about him, or was he only the boy from down the street, who could make a single stone skip a miraculous eleven times on the lake surface?

Galib was consumed entirely with thoughts of Chameli, and was relatively untouched by the fact that the world around him was collapsing. As they entered the new year, almost every evening his parents huddled with their friends. One or another guest would come in claiming an authentic inside scoop. Galib understood the situation only in its essence: Bangabandhu, a towering and much-beloved figure, whom Galib loved more than anything else for his signature smoking-pipe, had won the election, but the generals refused to hand over power. Galib scanned the front page photos every morning, leaders in talks, police beating crowds, but the infinite minutiae of how the great political impasse might be resolved lay beyond the powers of his concentration. There were too many points and counterpoints, and the intentions of adults were still mostly opaque to him.

The incessant talk of troubles in his house, no different from any other house at the time, penetrated his ears but not his heart, at least not yet. He heard his father say that when gossip becomes more trusted and urgent than the printed news, it was a time of great danger. He knew there were troubles on the street, millions had marched, and a few died. But all that occurred on other streets. Their little enclave, he felt, was specially protected, perhaps by some mythical beast that lurked in the bottom of the lake that girded their neighborhood.

Galib lived in unbearable impatience only for his next meeting with Chameli. The school shut down often due to protests, and on those mornings he pretended to study long enough to appease his mother, and then sneaked out to find Chameli.

The fact that till now they had never invited each other to their houses, he took as proof of their compact. He did not need her to say anything. It was enough that he was the only boy on the street with whom she talked. She had shown no interest to befriend any others. And while the boys teased him now and then, none of them had dared approach her either. They were no longer confined to the little corner of their lake. Sometimes they walked along its perimeter to far-off corners, and collected any fine stones, pieces of glass, or any suitable throwing material they discovered along the path.

Chameli told him how her mother had left her father for another man. That was when her father asked for a posting to East Pakistan. She was sad that her mother never wrote even to her. Galib was touched by this confidence and felt a little shallow that he did not have any sorrow of comparable moment to offer in return.

Galib had finally undergone a measure of cognitive adjustment in relation to Chameli. He could actually see her in full. She was no longer so bright an image that she appeared, even in his direct presence, only in fractals. He could still be surprised by different aspects of her beauty: the perfection of her ear lobes, a trill in her voice when she laughed out loud, the way the sun caught in her brown hair when it was untied. But, she was no longer a being of such distance and purity that he could not imagine touching her, or kissing her. In fact, that was something he desperately wanted to do. He certainly kept her safe from the impure thoughts that overcame him at night, sometimes even in broad daylight, like a horde of ruthless marauders. To quell the demands of these raiders in his blood, he sacrificed any image that would serve the moment's need—actresses in magazines, a friend's mother, on rare and befuddling occasions even Tabu's poor sister. But, Chameli was the only one he dreamed of kissing, if he only knew how.

They had such a lovely and easy bond. Could he risk disturbing it with a lunge, bound to be sudden and awkward, for a kiss? Like the period when he didn't know how to speak to her, this new longing thrust him into a new phase of despondency. Some days when they went out, he'd come ready to breach a new vale of intimacy, only to watch the moments pass with no real chance, or to witness with agonizing helplessness chances present and wasted.

"Why are you so serious today?" Chameli would ask.

It was winter and she wore her favorite sweater, a bright blue turtleneck. The sun was soft and came through the hanging branches to dapple their shoulders. Chameli walked with her arms folded across her small chest, with a measured pace that slowed him down.

"I'm not serious, I was just listening to you," Galib replied, with his eyes focused on the trail.

"I don't think so, you seem lost in your own thoughts," said Chameli.

"No, no, nothing, I was listening to you. Sometimes I just like to be quiet." He could not gauge what Chameli knew. To have such proximity to one's object of longing, but lack the temerity to transact fulfillment, what kind of curse was this? He was sure Chameli suspected nothing. How else could she be so carefree? Only a soul so free could derive such effervescent joy from the littlest things—a peacock feather discovered on their walks or a postcard from an aunt in Germany.

Did she have no thoughts or worries like his? What if he kissed her and she pushed him away in hurt dismay? Could he stand to be looked at by her in that manner? This was the crippling obstacle to his secret prayer.

So, some days he came out with neither thought nor intent of kissing her; that way at least he could enjoy the time with her in all its other aspects, like when they first met a few months ago.

It was in this fraught and frustrated period that Galib's father called him into the dining room one evening, while the usual guests thronged the drawing-room. His father, a riot with his friends, was somber with the family. To be called by him was rarely a promising turn of events for Galib.

There had hardly been any school the past month, so it could not be a matter of grades or discipline. Nor had he trespassed the few house rules set down by his parents. He made his own bed, came home by dusk. Was it the bidis then? Surely, the gardener wouldn't tell. And who else could have seen them? The cook, a friend? He cleaned his breath assiduously after each smoke.

In suspense, with timid steps he entered the room. Galib's father was seated at the head of their small dining table. From the adjacent room, through a door partly ajar, wafted in the noise and smoke generated by his father's friends. His father peered at him over his thick-rimmed glasses, with a smile that was meant to signal benevolence but smelled of menace.

"Tell me Galib, why don't you play football anymore?"

"It hurts my foot," replied Galib sullenly.

"We had another X-ray done, you know, and the doctor says there's nothing wrong," said his father.

"Still it hurts sometimes. Besides I like to read more nowadays."

"That's good, but you need exercise too," said his father. "A healthy body makes a healthy mind, you know?"

Galib was embarrassed to note that his father was faltering. Clearly this was not about sport, or books, or any other means of advancing his physical or mental well-being. These were not matters with which his father bothered too much directly or in details. Galib's father was diligent about providing house expenses, but its affairs were to his view entirely the provenance of his wife. On rare occasions she conscripted him into minor interventions of the present sort, which he suffered with thinning patience.

This conversation was about something else, but the man did not know how to segue into the real topic. As his father groped for a new opener, suddenly Galib realized with the electric intuition of a hunted animal what this meeting was about. He felt his limbs go numb, and he was sure he swayed. Or the room swayed, as his father's face grew larger and unrecognizable, mouthing the incantation of ancient priests before a ritual sacrifice. He heard the word "Punjabi" and something about not seeing that girl across the street at "a time like this."

Who was this man, and why was he talking to him? How had he never noticed what an uncomprehending brute he was? What did they have in common? The man was an alien. Why did he live in this house? The yellow overhead light made him feel nauseous. He said nothing to his father, but resolved in his heart to continue seeing Chameli. To leave this house as soon as he was old enough. He went to his room without dinner. Never had he felt such a cold wave of hatred towards another being as he did that night towards his father.

A day passed. Galib did not know how to broach the need to be discreet with Chameli. This delicacy held him back from seeing her. Their drawing-room window overlooked the street and her gate. From that window Galib noticed her dawdling at her gate in the afternoon. Clearly, she was waiting for him. She went inside and then came out again, a couple of times, before retiring for the evening. Two days later, when he spotted her next, she came out to hover at her gate, tucking a lock of stray hair behind her ear, and then walked up and down the street a few times before sauntering off in the direction of the lake. But she never looked up at his window.

After a week passed, Galib awoke one morning with only one thought on his mind: I must go see Chameli today. Since the closure of the schools, Galib had been placed under a home-study program by his mother. And though her supervision lacked the usual diligence, Galib spent his mornings trying to solve algebraic equations and reading des- ultorily about wildlife in Australia. He had learned that a country called Guinea held the largest reserves of bauxite in the world.

These days Galib knew he was expected only to put up the pre- tense of a study. Typically, Chameli and he rendezvoused in the late afternoon, which was the decent hour to go out for walks or to ride their bikes. But on this day, he devised an entirely new plan. Right after lunch he declared that he was going to see Tabu and boldly he made for the door. Once outside, slowly he crossed the street and looked up to see if anyone was peering out from his window. Satisfied that no one was watching him, he pushed open Chameli's gate and walked up to the portico of her house.

What if her father was home? Maybe he should have sent in the gardener to find out! But by now it was too late. He had already rung the bell. He noticed that pots of ferns had been placed on either side of the front steps in a half-hearted attempt at domesticity.

Chameli, looking older than usual in a floral kameez, opened the burnished black door herself and greeted him with a delighted surprise.

"Galib? Come inside," she said. She seemed not to notice that he had breached their silent pact not to visit each other's houses, but only to meet by the lake-side.

"Have you had lunch? Do you want a sandwich?" asked Chameli.

She led him into the drawing room. Like the entrance, this room too was not so much shabby, as incomplete: sofas and tables that did not complement each other, a TV in one corner, and various personal effects of both father and daughter—books, badminton racquets, office files—were strewn across the room. Galib sat down on the other end from Chameli in a large brown upholstered sofa. So this is where she lives! He felt sorry that there was no one, like his mother, to keep things tidy or bring any sense of décor to this place.

"I was wondering where you had been the last week. Why didn't you come out?"

"I was feeling a little sick," he lied.

"And you are fine now?"

"Yes, it wasn't anything much," he said. "Also, you know, my father worries a lot. He says times are bad, and we should not go out unless we need to."

"Even on this street? Nothing will happen here," said Chameli.

"I think so too, but you don't know my father. He worries a lot," said Galib, unable to bring himself anywhere close to the truth.

"My father says as soon as the army comes out, everything will quiet down."

"Maybe," said Galib, a little startled by her assurance. "No one really knows how it will all end, do they?"

This was not a conversation he wanted to continue with Chameli. He felt resentful that the preposterous world of adults was now imping-ing on their perfect plateau. They spoiled everything. That was all they were good for. He did not want them or their affair to enter between Chameli and himself. Not in this moment, not ever.

How easy it was to ignore his father's order! Why did he not come sooner? Why did they never visit each other's homes before? The room was dark, and only a soft afternoon sun filtered through the green drapes on the window. Chameli looked paler, and suddenly more unreachable than ever before. Still he was glad to be in her presence. Ever since the night of his father's injunction, he felt a dissonance deep within his being. A fear of loss before its occurrence was pressing on his mind. But as he sat across from her, the longer he sat, the more he felt restored to normalcy. He would visit her every day from now, he vowed to himself.

As she told him stories of her life back home, Chameli walked up to a decrepit boudoir as she told him stories of her life back home, to bring out an album. Once it was fetched, she came back and sat down beside him shoulder to shoulder. He could barely register either the images or any narratives about them. This was the house where we lived when Mum was still with us. And that was our dog, Speedy! Every time she turned towards him, the breath left him.

They sat with their legs supported against the coffee table. His thighs thin under dark blue jeans, and hers more defined and visible beneath the soft white cotton fabric of her salwar. Half the album opened on his lap and the other half on hers. He held up his side of the flap lightly with just his fingers. Every time she turned a page, her hand brushed lightly against his.

That's my aunt in Germany. She's married to a German. Never had he seen her face so close to his. Never had the perfume of her hair, or skin, or her clothes, so thoroughly invaded his lungs. And, he cursed himself bitterly for still not knowing if he should touch her face! He had never felt each moment last so long, while an afternoon passed so quickly.

In winter, at a certain point the afternoon light slips as if over a precipice, and the room grew suddenly darker. Even the chirping of the birds outside ceased for a moment. And then the infinite stillness of the moment was shattered by the harsh handling of cutleries in the kitchen. Chameli glanced at the wall clock and springing abruptly to her feet, she said, "I think my father will be back soon."

Galib was still holding the album on his lap. She did not say that he could not come again, but he knew that now it was time to go. Chameli stood at her door, her untied hair falling over one shoulder. Galib wondered when again they might sit so close together. A magical green winter light started to envelop the neighborhood. When he reached her gate and looked back over his shoulder, she was still at the door as if to palliate the invitation to leave.

Later that night, Galib was awakened, like the rest of the city, by the sound of rolling tanks and booming mortars. Gunfire rang out from different parts of tow—sounding by turns very far and shockingly near. The next morning the gardener arrived, without skull-cap, without glasses, his usually bleary eyes wide with terror. In a state of incoherence he talked of hundreds of people dead. Bodies in the university, bodies in New Market, bodies on the street. Bodies he had seen with his own eyes. He was leaving the city immediately and enjoined Galib's parents to do the same.

The troubles that had been talked about for months did not settle, instead they had escalated into war. Galib's parents talked in hushed tones about Tabu's father, a teacher in Dhaka University, who had not returned home the night before. All day long they went back and forth on options of evacuation. Galib felt more shame than fear. What a fool he had been all these months! How puerile, how oblivious. Obsessed only with the palpitation of his own little fantasies.

The next morning Galib and his parents fled the city. It all happened so quickly and quietly, there was no chance to see anyone. Not even to leave a message with the gardener. They escaped first to their home town, then to a village. They heard news like everyone else from passing refugees of great massacres, and by the end of monsoon, of thrilling reversals. In that time, Galib came to learn about history and politics, and came to care about what others cared about. Nine months later, at war's end, they came back to their home. The little blue house across the street was empty. His life before the war assumed the aura of a fairy tale. Chameli too became unreal again, but the ache she left behind in his heart felt true and permanent.

The Poetry Audition

Bahram and Jamshed were dressed alike as children because their father believed it to be the best way of preventing sibling rivalry. Rather than make them better friends though, their identical wardrobes led to some petty confusion. The brothers often wore each other's clothes by mistake. In family photographs of the time Bahram appeared scowling in shorts that hung down to his knees, while Jamshed smiled bravely in collars that nearly choked him.

Their sartorial semblance did not however extend to their character. Jamshed was a brash, bold, willful young boy. Bahram possessed the timidity of a provincial boy, a flaw that his mother could hardly tolerate. Jamshed was sent to a Cadet College, where he thrived, whereas it was a struggle to send Bahram to the posh day school a few streets from their home.

To break her son's debilitating shyness, Bahram's mother forced him to go to birthday parties and rewarded him by taking him to ice cream parlors and matinee shows, buying him toy cars and Lego sets. At night, she read him Russian fairy tales. But neither the forced socializing nor the ample gifts made any permanent mark on Bahram. He was immune to friendship. He regarded other guests at the parties with as much suspicion as he did the colored drinks and the loudly popping balloons. In exasperation, Bahram's mother resorted to rougher measures.

She urged him to go play in the neighborhood park. The first day she even walked him to the edge of it literally by the hand.

After she left, Bahram ventured as far as the main soccer field in the middle of the park with iron goalposts at each end. Having reached the boundary, though, he didn't know how to cross it. He wished that someone would ask him to join in the game, but such invitations were not abundantly forthcoming. At best, when the ball went out of the field on his side, he would receive a passing glance from the player who came out to fetch it. But this gave him an idea and he busied himself with his brand new soccer ball on the sidelines, occasionally allowing it to dart into the field. He ran after it hoping to create an occasion for striking up a friendship. But for the most part no one took any notice of him. When they did, the boys would stop playing–the man in possession stopping their official FIFA No. 5 black-and-white ball underfoot, a goalkeeper leaping up to grab the upper bar to have a stretch, and the other players using this unexpected moment of respite to sit or lie down–until Bahram collected his ball and returned to his outpost.

There were other boys who played in the side fields, but Bahram had grown a fixation for the main one. The boys who played there were quite indifferent to the sudden emergence of a lone spectator. Bahram persevered in his act until one day, when his ball went inside the field, a boy with a red armband picked it up and sent it flying with a kick into a nearby ditch. Everyone in the field laughed and Bahram too joined the laughter as though the joke was not at all on him, but on the muddied soccer ball. When he came home that day, smeared with mud and sweat, his mother said to him–, "Looks like you had a very good game today, Bahram." He nodded and affected more exhaustion than he felt, for he was sure that if he spoke his voice would quaver. After a wash, he came out to the verandah for tea. His mother asked him, "So, have you made some new friends?" By now more in control of himself, "Sure," he said.

A few days after Bahram's humiliation in the playground his brother Jamshed returned home for the Ramadan break from the Cadet

College. The first thing Jamshed wanted to know about as soon as he found himself alone with Bahram was the situation in the neighborhood park. How many groups were there, he asked, and who was in command of which? It had never occurred to Bahram to think of the playground in these terms. The mass of sweating, screaming, running hoodlums in the field had appeared to him as an amalgamated throng of hostile strangers. They were all together in a group and he was the lone outsider. Who would have thought that those boys might themselves be separated into rivaling factions? Jamshed used to be a regular at the field with a small team of his own, until he was sent away. Bahram was of course unable to answer any of Jamshed's questions and felt embarrassed about it. But he didn't hesitate to tell Jamshed about the incident at the field. Jamshed took him to the field that very afternoon to have the culprits identified.

"Him, that one with the red armband. He kicked my ball into the ditch," said Bahram pointing from afar at the worst offender.

"Him? That fat Bihari?" asked Jamshed, looking incredulously at Bahram.

Bahram felt the color rising to his cheeks and tried to shift the focus back to the culprit with, "Yes, that one. But I don't know his name."

"It's Asqari," said Jamshed and then added thoughtfully, "So they have taken over the main field."

The next day Jamshed forced Bahram to rummage with him in the garage all day, but refused to reveal for what he was looking. They collected all kinds of odd items and the next day they visited the neighborhood boys, whom Jamshed showered with the scavenged artifacts. He gave Badrul the chains and tires of a bicycle while the detached handles of the same vehicle went to Tulu. Afsar was puzzled with his toothless hairbrush, until Jamshed coolly pointed out that it had a mirror on the backside. When their stocks ran low, Jamshed bribed the darwans with cigarettes stolen from his father's drawer to gain access to other garages in the neighborhood. The finds were rich: skateboards without wheels, magnifying glasses gone foggy, gumboots with punctured soles, a German encyclopedia, several beautiful but empty bottles of wine and champagne and a set of false teeth with golden canines. These were freely distributed among the lesser members of the warring tribes. To win over the petty chieftains Jamshed parted with some of his most prized personal possessions – an American Indian costume, a Nepalese dagger with a leather case, and an authentic general's badge.

One day they found a broken viewfinder that Bahram wanted to keep, and Jamshed agreed to let him have it. But when they arrived at Montu's, Jamshed suddenly fished out the viewfinder and said, "Look Montu, what Bahram found for you."

Although the same snowy landscape appeared no matter how many times one clicked the viewfinder, Montu seemed terribly pleased. When they came out from Montu's, Bahram looked accusingly at Jamshed and said, "You said I could have that. Why did you give it away?"

"The damn thing was broken anyway. What did you want it for?" laughed Jamshed.

"But still," complained Bahram, having formed a sentimental attachment to the object in the short span of time between its discovery and its dispensation. "You said it was mine."

One afternoon, a few days later, Jamshed took Bahram and his red football to the park a little before four. Jamshed had learned that the Biharis always came to the field at that hour. Their numerousness and fierce group loyalty made them unassailable. Since the others had to clear the field when the Biharis showed up, they tried to play as much as they could in the main field before four.

But on this day, the park was surprisingly empty. Two half-naked but robust slum children ran around the park with their sticks and hoops. Except the metal ringing on the cement pathway nothing disturbed the peace of the shady green field.

Jamshed seemed not to notice the uncanny silence that had descended on the park and asked Bahram to throw him the ball. He blocked the ball with his chest and then caught it with his knees before it fell to the ground. No matter whether he kicked the ball with the front, back or side of his foot, it came back to Bahram with deadly accuracy. Bahram threw the ball very high to Jamshed, but no matter how high it was thrown Jamshed headed it back unflinchingly.

Bahram regarded his brother's feat with proud astonishment. As Bahram watched the ball went up to the sky, it shrank smaller, and before it had time to come down he heard a whistle. It came from one of the Bihari boys, most of whom were still busy putting down their bags and flasks. As always they had come directly from school and in their white uniforms looked, though it wasn't the season for it, like a professional cricket team. Instead of heading the ball back Jamshed took it in his arms, while Bahram shuffled up closer to him.

"Hey you two, take your game to the side," said the fat Bihari as one by one his players filed onto the field.

"But we haven't finished playing yet," said Jamshed.

"Well, finish playing over there," said the fat one as he strode up to Jamshed, his finger raised, even after he had finished speaking, in the intended direction.

"Why don't you play over there?" Now Jamshed raised his finger in the same direction and left it that way.

The Bihari didn't answer. Some of his teammates started crowding around him, murmuring with some disdain, "Is there a problem?"

"You should go there because we always play here," explained the fat Bihari.

"But why should we play in the outfield when we got here first?"

"They got here first." repeated the Bihari turning to his fellows. A ripple of laughter went around their circle.

"Should we carry them out?"

"No, let me get them the hoops from those kids."

"Jamshed, let's just go over there," murmured Bahram. But Jamshed quieted him with an assuring squeeze on the shoulder.

"Look," said the Bihari with the tolerance of a benevolent tyrant, "We need the main field. There's so many of us, but only two of you."

"Yeah," said Jamshed, "But the others are coming."

Badrul, Tulu, Afsar and Montu along with the other neighborhood kids stepped out from behind the trees on Jamshed's side of the field wielding cricket bats and steel pointed wickets. Badrul was the only one not carrying any unseasonal sporting equipment; he held a cycle chain slung carelessly over his shoulders.

"Okay, okay," said the Bihari, "You play outside today. We'll play there tomorrow."

"You'll play there tomorrow," said Jamshed, foot resting on his little red ball, "But you'll also play there today." His team began to form a circle around the Biharis.

The leader of the Biharis looked around despairingly at his own teammates. When no one on his side spoke up, he began again–,"Okay, okay," wetting his lips quickly, "Okay, I'll tell you what..."–but before he could finish speaking Jamshed pounced on him.

"No I'll tell you what, you fat slob." Jamshed punched him and the boy fell to the ground, covering his face, emitting fearful utterances in his own language. Jamshed sat on the fallen boy's chest, and landed quick but heavy blows on his covered face, shoulders, arms.

The teammates of the boy thought to be Bihari were too stunned by the suddenness and ferocity of Jamshed's attack to move. And when some of them tried to back out, Jamshed's team held them in with a barricade of bats and wickets. Jamshed rose from his opponent's chest, feet planted firmly on either side of his fallen nemesis, and proclaimed to the assembled crowd–,"From today this park is ours. We will play here whenever we like and you will play on the outside. You can play in the middle too if you join my team. I'll be the captain of the new team, even when I'm not here..."

Bahram was already impressed by Jamshed's crewcut, his blue-gray uniform, his range of acquaintances, and sportsmanship. But now, after the reclamation of the field, Jamshed became in his eyes as amazing as any bona fide conquistador. From among all the members of his new team, Jamshed selected the best talents to form the main eleven. But once he got to the extras people with non-sporting talents started making the team. Afsar was included because he proved to be an unfailing agent of contraband items—nicotine, alcohol, pornography. Not that his supplies necessarily ensured enjoyment, because once he brought a pound of tobacco but couldn't find a pipe. Tulu became an extra for he had permanent access to a car and another boy had unlimited credit at the local chatpatiwalla's. Someone's father owned a Chinese restaurant and another's uncle a movie house. Even Asqari—the fat Bihari, who, they found out, like most of his teammates, was actually not Bihari at all, but from other parts of India—made the team because when they weren't amusing themselves with free meals or movies, or when it was too hot to drive around the city they could peacefully soak inside or sting one another with wet towels around Asqari's kidney-shaped swimming pool. Jamshed, though only a few years older than Bahram, already possessed not only a taste for the high life but also a knack for inducing its magical manifestation. He also showed an early streak of nepotism by including his singularly untalented brother into this inner circle. At night when they talked across the narrow gap between their beds Jamshed would promise to make Bahram the plenipotentiary of his office when he left for school.

Their parents were cheered to see the impact Jamshed had on Bahram. They thought it might be good for the boys to be together. They considered sending Bahram to the Cadet College or keeping Jamshed at home, and after a month of nightly and circular debates they decided to keep Jamshed at his school and Bahram at home. The boys had to be sent to the kind of schools where they would do their best. The day before he left, Jamshed pulled Bahram aside to explain why, contrary to his promises and earlier plans, he had to put Asqari in charge of the team. "You understand, you are too young to be made captain, or even vice-captain," said Jamshed, although he himself was a bit younger than a lot of the boys in their group. "No one would listen to you, yet." Bahram was easily persuaded and didn't mind the slow fall in his status after Jamshed's departure.

Whenever the team split up now to play practice matches, Asqari and Badrul led the two halves. If they had an odd-numbered gathering to pick from, Bahram would be left hanging in the middle. One of the two captains would invariably say to the other–, "You guys take him, we'll play with one less." Sometimes this magnanimous offer to play with fewer players was countered with–, "But we had him in our team yesterday."

Bahram's recoil from the park was so gradual as to be almost unnoticeable. He hardly minded himself, as new interests claimed him. Grandfather's library of books became his hunting ground. He had always had a fascination for that room, though as a child it was forbidden to him–, "Don't disturb Grandfather." Yet, Bahram would tiptoe up the staircase to the corner room that overlooked the back garden, slowly open the door, and wait for Grandfather to look up from his thick, heavy, musty-smelling books to beckon him inside. Grandfather would make him an airplane with a scribbled over yellow writing paper. Bahram would fling it in the air and chase it around, while Grandfather became absorbed again in his abstractions. As a child, Bahram loved the mysterious smell of sweet tobacco and leather that enshrouded Grandfather wherever he went and hung heavy in his library.

For a few years, Bahram had ceased to visit the room, since he had become too old for paper planes. Now, old enough for the attractions of the room, Bahram was entranced by its dark coolness and quietness. The shades were always drawn, allowing only geometric slices of afternoon light to filter in through the slats, and an ancient fan rotated slowly, tiredly to the accompaniment of a soothing, metronomic noise. Grandfather had become too old to spend the whole day in that room. He came up still for a morning of perusal with his magnifying glass. But while he slumbered after lunch in the afternoons, Bahram made the place his own.

Grandfather was delighted to know that there was someone in the house to go on caring for his books, but Bahram's father worried about his son's effete tastes. He was too refined to be openly forbidding or even discouraging.

Back home early some afternoons, Bahram's father would come up to the library to find his son slouching with a book.

"Reading?"

"Hm."

"It was such a lovely afternoon outside. If you are going to stay in, turn the lights on at least."

"Hm."

"What are you reading?"

"Gibbon."

"Again?"

Bahram would look up, trying hard to hide his annoyance, and searching an answer to a question that to his mind had no meaning. Every time his father found him with a book that he thought was excessively scholarly or literary, his consternation would heighten.

"Reading's a good habit," he would tell his wife. "But too much of it can be crippling. There was a boy with us who read all the time–Marx and what not. Thick glasses; he was so serious that he wouldn't even say 'hi' to me or anyone on the street. One opened conversations with him by asking what he thought of dialectic materialism. He really did know a lot. But never came to anything much. He's a clerk now in some office. And writes little stories for papers."

Bahram's mother would smile at her husband's exaggerated fears for their son's future. "Maybe he'll be famous some day," she would respond.

"Who? Bahram?"

"No, your friend."

"You may think it's funny, but I'm telling you, books can be dangerous. They've spoiled so many good talents."

"Oh, you worry too much," his wife would say. "I'm sure it's just a phase."

Both parents were lulled into believing this consoling fib, since every break when Jamshed came home, Bahram would visit the park more than he ever did on his own. This small departure from his sedentary routines, they took as a sign of hope. If it weren't for these seasonal excursions prompted by Jamshed's visit, Bahram might have completely lost touch with his childhood gang. The gang had splintered back into several factions when Tulu left with some of the newer boys to create a team of his own; they wanted to play cricket all year round. Most of the older friends—Badrul, Afsar, Montu, and, surprisingly, Asqari had, however, stayed with Jamshed's team.

Distance had not diminished the intimacy between the two brothers, but their friendship had changed. Bahram no longer needed Jamshed's protection, nor did he rely exclusively on Jamshed for the sake of his entertainment. Jamshed, on the other hand, increasingly depended on Bahram for help with his studies. Bahram had earned enough double promotions and Jamshed lost enough years that in spite of two years' age difference, Bahram was now the same grade as Jamshed, and equally skilled in solving geometry theorems and writing creative essays.

In their looks too they had grown remarkably apart. Even his own clothes hung too loose on Bahram, blue-green veins showing under his pale skin. Jamshed had the complexion of damp earth. He could look disjointed owing to too much height, but whenever he was put to the test he displayed extraordinary strength and coordination.

In the afternoons Jamshed went out swishing a tennis racquet from side to side. Bahram spent his afternoons either in Grandfather's study or at Uncle Haider's, whose house was a veritable dormitory of derelicts. Addicts of every kind were received there with open arms, and Bahram was delighted to be accepted in this circle of elders. There was always a strong supply of well brewed tea, filter-less cigarettes, and even an occasional puff of dope. But Bahram's addiction was a good adda.

Uncle Haider could hold forth on any number of subjects: the treatises of Ibn-al-Arabi or the poetry of Gabriela Mistral, the habits of Australian sloths and court rituals of the Safavis—for him to know about anything it was only necessary for the subject to be sufficiently odd, obscure or useless. Sometimes, after his tennis, Jamshed came to look for Bahram at Uncle Haider's. Even when he knew Bahram was there, he couldn't always readily identify his brother's smoke shrouded figure. "God, don't you guys ever air this room?" he'd say, as he left with Bahram.

This routine became very common the winter after they both graduated from college, with very different results. One evening, when they walked back from Uncle Haider's, much later than usual, Rauf the servant informed them that their father was looking for them.

"What exactly did he say? Was he just asking if we were around or did he say he wanted to see us?" asked Jamshed.

"He said to go see him as soon as you came in."

"How did he say it? Did he sound angry?" asked Bahram.

"No, he just said, 'Where are they? Tell them to come see me.'"

"You have any idea what this is about?" Bahram asked Jamshed as they went to see their father after dinner.

"Where have you boys been all day? Come on, sit down." Their father looked earnest, but showed no signs of discontentment. He lay in his bed, propped up by a cloud of soft pillows, Rauf massaging his feet with oil.

"That's enough," he said to Rauf, waving him away. "So where have you been—at the park?"

"No we were at Uncle Haider's."

"There again. No wonder you smell of cigarettes. Anyway, the reason I called you, now that you have both graduated, you must decide what you're going to do."

"I want to become a Professor of Philology," said Bahram, without a moment's hesitation.

Their father, presumably thinking it safer simply to move on, and in hopes presumably of a saner response, asked Jamshed, "What about you?"

Jamshed had gone pale from the moment he saw what the purpose of this audience was. He knew that the session was well overdue and he had rehearsed clever little speeches in anticipation of it from the day he came back home. But those dazzling little rhetorical vignettes that he had performed with so much panache for Bahram behind closed doors, completely eluded him now. He cast one last despairing glance in Bahram's direction before opening his mouth. "I–I want to be a poet."

Their father was at once dumbfounded.

"Bahram, I always knew was a fool," said their father with a deep deliberation. "What the hell is wrong with you?"

He massaged the back of his neck vigorously as he always did when overcome with anger or stress.

As Bahram and Jamshed both sat in petrified silence, readying themselves for more vitriol and anguish to pour forth from their surprised father, suddenly the man changed tack. In a softer, but challenging voice he asked Jamshed, "Exactly how do you intend to go about becoming a poet?"

Bahram, though not surprised, was pained by the ensuing interchange. He felt largely responsible for the strait that Jamshed seemed hell-bent on getting deeper into. Bahram had introduced Jamshed to poetry. He had always felt a strong compulsion to share with Jamshed the latest source of his own excitements. But in this particular case he was also motivated by the desire to mitigate—with a gentle dose of culture—Jamshed's lack of sophistication, if not downright uncouthness, in thought and feeling, which he knew was a natural consequence of long stays in the Cadet College and overexposure to ruffians.

Bahram worried that getting Jamshed to read the poems at all would be the hardest part. But Jamshed proved infinitely amenable to the suggestion. Bahram started him on some of the older local talents—Tagore, Nazrul, Satyendranath Dutta, and, of course, Sukanta. Then he brought him to the Big Five—the great modernist pioneers of the '30s—Jibanananda Das, Amiya Chakravarty, Sudhindranath Dutta, Buddhadev Basu, and Bishnu Dey. Bringing Jamshed to the Bengalis before the foreigners, Bahram later realized, was a mistake. Because now Jamshed was excited to recognize traces of the Bengali poets in the writings of Mallarmé, Valéry and Arragon, or Pound, Eliot, and Auden. To Jamshed locating influences was a highly sophisticated form of literary discussion and he could not stop talking about the Bengalis' impact on world poetry. When Bahram tried to correct him he would say smugly, "Bahram, don't think you know everything."

This was the first time that Bahram noticed Jamshed's peculiar tendency to become attached to certain ideas that pleased him. And Jamshed might have clung to his deluded notions about the directions of cultural influence, if one day at the end of his patience, Bahram hadn't grabbed Jamshed by the shirtfront and yelled into his face, "Jamshed, Mallarmé died before Jibanananda Das was born. Mallarmé died before *any* of these guys were born. Mallarmé died in fucking 1898! He couldn't have read any of these guys even if he had wanted to, even if he had known Bengali, because not even Bengal knew of them at the time. So don't ever again talk about influences."

Nothing dampened Jamshed's passion for poetry. He went around almost in a trance reciting lines from his favorite poems–:"I should have been a pair of ragged claws, scuttling the floors of the silent seas." Bahram found it acutely funny that a robust soul like Jamshed should be so deeply moved by lines expressing a desire for a crustacean existence and resolved to do all he could to sustain Jamshed's enthusiasm for poetry.

Bahram worried that Jamshed might suddenly grow tired of these poems and continued to bring him new material. As it happened, Jamshed showed no inclination at the time for the newer poems with which Bahram sought to retain his interest; he just read and reread the poets he already liked. Problems along these lines Bahram had anticipated; but what he hadn't foreseen was that Jamshed might start writing poems of his own.

Jamshed was so deeply convinced of the merit of his poetry, that when he showed them to his brother, Bahram didn't have the heart to offer his honest opinion. Around the same time Jamshed also began to discover new poets on his own. And when he brought home some Kaikobad and Sufia Kamal, Bahram realized that his brother was as vulnerable to truly bad poetry as he was to truly great poetry. Jamshed's graduation was a year away, and he informed Bahram in a letter–written entirely in verse–that he had made his life's decision: he was going to be a poet. Bahram saw this as a dangerous and unfortunate development, which he felt incumbent on himself to reverse.

As always Bahram pursued his goal by subtle inducements. He affected great indifference to the subject of poetry. He cancelled his subscriptions to the literary journals and wrote to Jamshed saying that he didn't feel like reading poems very much anymore. Jamshed wrote back, "You have a pedantic mind, which is why you can amass information and say clever things about anything you read but you don't know what it is to feel strongly."

When Jamshed came home after graduation, Bahram took more extreme measures. He gave away his poetry books, saying that they cluttered his room. The day he gave away an early edition of *Dhusar Pandulipi*, Jamshed asked him ruefully, "Why did you give that away? I thought you said I could have it."

Bahram resigned himself to secret despair. And as they sat before their father he told himself that he had tried all along to save Jamshed from such a scene. But since Jamshed had refused to take hints, he would have to hear it from someone.

"I want to be a poet," Jamshed said again.

"Where, where do you even get these ideas? You have been reading Bahram's books as well, haven't you?"

"Bahram has nothing to do with this. I want to be a poet on my own."

"Jamshed has actually had this interest for quite a while now," said Bahram.

"Is this what they teach in the Cadet Colleges nowadays–to become a poet?"

"No, this is an interest I developed outside of College."

"Haider has been giving you ideas, hasn't he?" Uncle Haider, like all intellectuals, was held in contempt by their father and tolerated only for the sake of kinship.

"No, Uncle Haider has nothing to do with it either. No one influenced me. It's my own interest."

"So, how does one go about becoming a poet? What do you propose to do now?"

"I guess I'll get a job at a paper or something, and write poetry."

"Jamshed, Jamshed. Who's going to give you a job at a paper? How much do you think you'd make at a job like that? Or from your books, if you had any published? It's the kind of thing you can do in Europe or America–in more civilized countries, where there are millions of educated people, thousands of readers. No one gives a damn here about poets and such. You must have a solid career–a title–be a doctor, or an engineer, a barrister, or a colonel."

"I don't care for titles and positions."

"But you must. Titles for a man are like handles for a teacup. Without it no one will pick you up."

"I don't care if they do."

"That's what you think now."

"That's what I'll always think."

"No! That's where you are wrong. You can think now that you'll always think that way because you don't know what it's like to not have any prestige or privilege." Bahram braced himself for a familiar tirade along the lines of what-I-had-to-do-when-I-was-your-age and don't-flush-it-away-now-because-when-I'm-gone followed by a lecture on the importance of availing oneself of opportunities and cultivating connections. "You think at your age I didn't want to be a poet or an actor or something glamorous like that?" Their father couldn't afford the delusions of a dandy; he had studied entirely on scholarships. "I used to stay up nights worrying how I would put Haider and Hannan through school if father died." Their grandfather had become a Public Notary after years of serving the British Government and was considered a modest success because he had been able to maintain that post until the time of his retirement. "You didn't see the things I saw growing up, that's why you don't appreciate what a privilege it is to be able to hold the jobs you call *boring.*" He was out of his bed now, pacing up and down the length of the room. "You think I went into making steam boilers at your age because it was fun? When I went into the boiler business, no one in this country knew what to do with them." Their father's generation allegedly still worried about doing things for the country. Developing it, modernizing it. "We need people who can make roads and bridges, buildings and culverts. What's another poet? What can people do with words?–Nothing, nothing at all." They didn't know anything–he told them–about the indignities of waiting in corridors to bribe crooked bureaucrats for the signing of petty contracts. "At your age, you see the glamour but not the grit of things. You want to do something great? You want to make history? Well, let me tell you something–: I was the first person in this country to export steam boilers, *that's* history."

Their mother came in to find out what all the commotion was about. A bigger pragmatist than her husband, she said–, "So what if he wants to write poems. Let him, he's young yet. He'll find out if it's something he's really meant to do."

"No, to have a proper career he must start now. You always told me to be lenient with Haider. Look what's come of that."

"Oh, was I the one who was lenient with Haider? Who was giving him fat allowances, because they wanted their kid brother to have the things that they didn't have?"

As their parents plunged into a pet debate, Bahram and Jamshed were able to get away for the evening.

"You could have said something," muttered Jamshed as they stepped out of the room.

"Say what? I didn't think you'd bring it up so tactlessly. You need to prepare people for news like that."

"You could have told him how good my poems are. You could have–"

"Look, let's not start fighting ourselves, what we need is a new strategy."

"Bahram. You don't actually believe that I'll make it as a poet, do you?" This was not the first time Jamshed had put the question to Bahram, and while neither of them ever tried to specify what would constitute "making it as a poet," Bahram answered as he always did, "The problem you see, Jamshed, is that you don't know if you've really made it as a poet until a century has gone by. So in a sense, we will never know. If you write, you must do so on faith."

"That's what I intend to do."

"Yes, but you must also think of pragmatics a little. Maybe you should think of it as a part-time thing. Get a real job, as father was saying, and write in the evenings."

"Devotion can't be part-time," Jamshed replied grimly.

Although they escaped the evening's diatribe midway, they knew that more might be coming. Jamshed's professional choice was not solely a matter of his personal decision. Or even his immediate family's. Anyone with the potential of a future patriarch–like Jamshed–became a subject of the whole extended family's vigilance. As news got around, words of dim regret and disapproval poured in from the wide circle of dim-witted relatives. Jamshed solicited Uncle Haider's help to persuade his father, though Bahram questioned the strategic soundness of this move. But Uncle Haider, much sharper than either Bahram or Jamshed in handling what he called "the Byzantine mechanics of the family," roped in Uncle Hannan for the mediation. Uncle Hannan, on better terms with their father, persuaded the recalcitrant parent to withhold judgment on Jamshed, at least until he had had a chance to prove his talent.

Their father called them up again two days later, "I take it you two were behind Hannan's visit. But I don't want to be unfair. I am not going to be the judge of Jamshed's poetry. Other people will do it. All the relatives are coming on Friday. Jamshed will read them his poems. Mawlana Arakan Khan, who is a very learned man and knows more than any of us about poetry, Eastern or Western, has graciously accepted Mannan Dada's invitation to come to this little affair."

Apparently, the two brothers and Uncle Haider were not the only ones thinking strategically. The news of their great-uncle Mannan Dada's attendance was quite alarming, to say nothing of an exalted stranger such as the Mawlana. The bench was now heavily stacked against the defendant.

"This would have never happened if Grandfather was still alive," murmured Jamshed.

"A lot would not be happening if he were still alive," agreed Bahram ruefully.

Since Mannan Dada had lost neither his wealth nor his wits, even in his eighties he held tremendous sway over the entire clan. This arch-patriarch had long been held at bay while their own grandfather was alive, since the two men had disagreed violently on everything since their youth. One of them had chosen to go to the Presidency College to read Keats, the other had opted for Aligarh to become a modern Muslim. Ever since Grandfather's death, however, Bahram and Jamshed's father had gravitated towards this other elder. Although their father didn't share the elder's piety, temperamentally they were kindred conservatives.

Whenever older family members convened to discuss some important issue Mannan Dada sat in as the chief arbiter. Uncle Haider had termed this informal institution the Council of Elders. The Council met most frequently to discuss weddings, less frequently but with more enthusiasm to settle divorces or property disputes, and had the highest attendance for scandalous issues—abortion or adultery. Sometimes the Council convened for rather light-hearted matters—to endorse the naming of a child or to condemn some renegade's renunciation of the family name. But rarely was the Council brought together by a controversy related to art. There was the incident with Uncle Hannan, who had run away to Bombay to become a movie star. After he was captured and delivered home by relatives in India, the Council had ordered his head be shaved and when his hair grew back to a decent length he was married off. Head shavings and sudden marriages had been a popular and potent means of controlling aberrant behavior only a generation before.

The Council had never invaded their home in quite this capacity, certainly not while Grandfather was alive. But times had changed.

On Friday evening Uncle Haider and Uncle Hannan were the first to arrive in the small red Fiat of which they both claimed ownership. All the relatives showed up shortly after, in time for the Maghreb prayers. But the reading was held up by the delayed arrival of Mawlana Arakan Khan. The Mawlana was an old teacher of grandfather's, and himself a protégé of a historical figure like Sayeed Qutub. This was an association he had formed during his student days at Al Azhar in Cairo, but following the execution of his mentor he fled Egypt to form alliances with the followers of Maududi. He had by now acquired such an aura of ancientness that people felt free to say he had been associated with not just the likes of Maududi and Sayeed Qutub, but figures much older than them. He was said to have been one of the first discoverers of Lalon Fakir, to have known the Sultan of Turkey, and to have been a tutor of the last Moghul. He was old enough that almost any kind of claim could be made about his connections. Angels, spirits, prophets, and departed greats of all manner were thought to hold regular court with him.

The very sight of him–six-feet tall, enrobed in regal white, with a soft white beard and intense, small blue eyes–seemed so majestic and holy, that it was bound to extract a certain amount of almost genetically encoded reaction of pious submission from even the most hardened apostates.

The Mawlana arrived with his usual retinue of petty clerics–all of them robed and bearded like the Mawlana himself. But what in the Mawlana's case gave a sense of nobility, suggested in his followers only meanness. The smell of the cheap attar, the black kohl on their eyelashes, everything was repulsive. Most of them had tinged their beards red with mehendi. These reddened beards not only indicated their religiosity, but for the doubters they also served the purpose of a political barometer. The more the country tilted towards orthodoxy, the redder became the beards.

By the time all the guests were satiated with food and banter and ready to settle down–some with tea cups, others with their pipe and cheroot–it was close to midnight.

Jamshed had lost ten pounds in one week. He looked pale and ter-rified. Over the course of the week, Jamshed's until now unshakeable faith in his own work had become severely reduced. No matter how many times Bahram told him–, "Don't worry, they'll love it–,"Jamshed would solemnly shake his head and say–, "Maybe I should change the line about the cloud-seared moon."

Two days before the reading Jamshed came to Bahram and said, "Which poems do you think I should read? These prose poems are obvi-ously better, but maybe they'd prefer verses."

Bahram propped himself up on his elbows and looked at Jamshed intently. "I can't choose," said Jamshed with a despairing smile. "What should I read?"

"You should read Baudelaire and Rimbaud," Bahram said with a conspiratorial smile.

Jamshed looked at him unsurely. "Look," said Bahram, "Your po-ems are very good, but why take chances? You can't go wrong with Baudelaire and Rimbaud."

"Where are we going to find translations?" said Jamshed, still un-convinced. "What if they recognize the stuff?"

"They won't recognize anything," said Bahram. "I'll translate them for you myself."

The idea appealed to Jamshed and he lay flat on the floor next to Bahram's bed, reading and suggesting changes as Bahram passed him each sheet of the translated poems and finally persuaded him to throw in a few lines of Eliot. Although Jamshed did not doubt the greatness of the poems he held in his hands, as he stood in front of the Council, his mouth still went dry. The reading progressed. Tea cups were refilled. Pipes relit. Trays full of samosas and halvas passed around the room, and Jamshed began to get into the rhythm of his recitation. Yes, this was great poetry, he was sure. He felt inspired and forgot that what he read was not his own creation. He began to improvise, calling the readers hypocrites—which was in the original—but also comparing them to a pair of ragged claws. Lines like—, "life, what"—came out of his mouth with native fluidity. He threatened to show his readers the fireworks of hell in a handful of dust. The elders listened gravely, intently. Many were sleepy. They would have fallen asleep a long time ago, if they weren't jarred every so often by unexpected epithet-like phrases issuing forth from Jamshed's mouth. The reading lasted over two hours and the Council went into conference when Jamshed finished. It was past midnight.

Bahram and Jamshed sat outside the drawing room. Jamshed was still agitated from his evening's performance. His color was high and eyes bright. Bahram kept assuring him that the reading had been marvelous. A little while later they were called back into the drawing room. Mawlana Arakan sat flanked by their grandfather and Mannan Dada. Grandfather, usually the most venerable member of the household, looked like a child next to his mentor and uncle. Their father sat right behind the Mawlana. The others formed a circle. Bahram and Jamshed went and stood in the middle of the room.

"What does *he* want to be?" The Mawlana asked, pointing to Bahram. His voice was so meek and high pitched, it sounded like an old slow speed recording.

"He's the younger one," their father said. "He wants to be a professor, of philology."

"There's no harm in becoming a professor. The income is not so great. Especially for a subject like philology. But there's no harm in it," said the Mawlana, Mannan Dada nodding. It seemed as if Jamshed's choice was so extravagant, that Bahram's audacity had become forgivable.

The Mawlana held the brothers in a deep gaze and then began reciting, first in the original Persian and then in Bengali:

"They say the Lion and the Lizard keep
The Courts where Jamshed gloried and drank deep
And Bahram, that great hunter–The Wild Ass
Stamps o'er his Head, but cannot break his Sleep.

"Do you know who wrote that? That's Omar Khayyam. When I was your age, his quatrains used to haunt me. But you don't read Omar Khayyam anymore. You know neither your own tradition well, nor that of the West. If you did you'd notice how close the sentiment here is to "Ozymandias." But you probably don't even know what that is. You do? That's good. They tell me Romanticism has gone out of fashion. When I was young it was everything. But nothing impressed us as the Sufis did. How we used to shudder at Omar Khayyam's hedonistic audacity. It made us tremble in delight, in fear. Poetry was not something we read carelessly. The greatest mystics were borne on its wings to the state of *f'ana*–the fearsome pleasure of uniting with the One, the only One. But the careless mind could be led astray by its superficial charms. You found or lost your Soul reading the likes of Sadi and Hafez, Rumi and Suhrawardy.

"In your poems, there is so much passion, yet so little soul. Why, why does it ring so hollow? Is it because you shallowly imitate the Western poets? Why do you write about despair and nihilism? Their history is not your history. What is all this talk of boredom and isolation? Why do you sing songs of lament–it is the century of their defeats, their moral disasters. But you are so misguided by your modern education," this he said casting a reproachful glance at their father, who hung his head low with a penitent's humility, "that it would not be fair for me to blame you."

"I have discussed your interests with your elders and we don't think you should spoil the opportunity to start a good career. You must pursue a career in something that you have manifest talent and training for. Therefore, it is the wish of your elders, Jamshed, that you go into the army. We all think you will have a bright future there. This is of course not to say that you should give up poetry. On the contrary, it is a noble instinct to have, one that should be cherished, perhaps cultivated further, with proper guidance. But it should not be done carelessly or without proper guidance. I have therefore also arranged with your father's permission for you to read with one of my brightest disciples, Hasib al-Imam. He will come every Friday morning from now. You'll read together, then go for the prayers. Hasib is an expert of Persian poetry, both modern and ancient. You will, of course, start with the classics—Firdausi, perhaps. And this will give you the background you lack."

The Mawlana leaned back in his chair, drawing the hem of his caftan over his lap. The session was over. Bahram and Jamshed left the room with a quick and respectful salaam to the Mawlana.

Bahram and Jamshed collapsed in the dining room. The table had been cleared, while the reading was in progress, but the stale smell of the dinner lingered in the air. The brothers sat in silence, made all the more pronounced by the indistinct hum coming from the drawing room.

Uncle Haider stopped in. "Jamshed, why so glum? Worse things happen to people than having to read Persian poetry." Uncle Haider slapped Jamshed on the shoulder and complimented him on his reading "Sounded familiar, but these new ones were much better than your earlier ones. What can you do with the wrong audience?"

Jamshed said nothing. Many of the other guests peeked in, some coming in to shake hands with Bahram and Jamshed or to ruffle their hair, by way of saying farewell. The servants wanted to know if Jamshed wanted to eat now, since he had passed on dinner before. But Jamshed didn't want anything. After the last guest left, their mother brought him a plate of food, which Jamshed left untouched. The lights went out in the drawing room, they heard their father's footsteps going up the stairs. He never came in. The servants turned in a little later. The night watchman's whistle rang outside. Jamshed sat quietly. Bahram offered oblique words of consolation, "Many great poets went to the army, you know. Our own Nazrul fought in Turkey during the Second World War. Baudrillard was polishing cannons in the First–"

"Don't you think I've had enough lectures for one night, professor?" That silenced Bahram, but Jamshed too kept quiet. Bahram, the artful malingerer, who had always been able to slink out of places, couldn't come up with any excuse to leave. Jamshed sat in his corner and, with his hound-dog eyes held Bahram at his, even after it grew light out, even after the first rickshaw bells sounded on the streets.

Losing Ayesha

The first time I was ever sad, I mean truly sad, the kind of sadness that wipes out all the light from the world and you're sure that the heavy curtain that has descended all around you will never lift again, occurred when I was seven years old. The event was of course a ludicrously small one. It was a winter's afternoon, and I had been asked to go take a nap, after which I'd go play in the front lawn. A simple routine of our regimented little household: wake up at seven; breakfast of eggs and toast with a big mug of Ovaltine; play in the lawn at four-thirty; watch TV for an hour before bed. My mother magically appeared at every transition point of the day to ensure I was sticking to the schedule.

We lived at the time in a small, symmetrical, one-storey, red-brick house in Banani. The area was still pristine. Most of the plots were empty. Foxes howled at night in the nearby grave-yard. Our house was uncommonly framed by a lawn both in the back and in the front. The back lawn was packed with fruit trees. My father had planted a swing and a see-saw set amid the rows of leafy palms and green bananas. But the evenings filled the place with shadows and, to my seven-year-old mind, ghouls and serpents. Even in broad daylight I did not fully trust that place and never went there alone.

The front lawn, which felt huge to me, but I discovered to be nothing but a strip when I went back there years later, was my playground. To run around in that lawn with a No. 3 football, light enough for my small feet, was all I lived for. My best friend, really my only friend, Raqib, arrived at four-thirty every day, in an ill-fitting red Liverpool jersey, and we'd set up goal posts at one end with half-sized bricks. Little fanatics that we were, we did not switch to cricket in winter like the other kids. We forced the sweet, compliant, overweight cook, Moti Mama, to stand in for goalkeeper. We ran all over the lawn, trampling the flower-beds that lined it, scraping our shins on thorny bushes. We kicked each other, cried foul, and appealed to the goalie, who doubled as referee. We ran as hard as our little lungs allowed with the bloody intent to send a lancing shot past the flailing keeper. Every even match ended with a penalty kick-off. In our world, there were no draws; only winners and losers. Given the intensity of these jousts, you can imagine how important each day's contest felt to us, especially if one had lost the previous day. Until the next combat, the only thing that reverberated in our minds was the mistake that permitted the undeserving rival to score a winning goal. One lived only for a chance to correct that mistake.

I can no longer remember if the afternoon I am talking about was loaded with any great expectations of a rematch. All I recall is that my mother sent me off to nap, and amazingly that she, who was more precise than the hands of any ticking clock, failed to awaken me in time to go play with Raqib. When I awakened on my own, it was practically dusk outside. The purple rays of a setting sun tinged the western sky with a farewell signature that told me, This afternoon will never come again! That was all I understood, and I was bereft.

Why did my mother not wake me up? Why not Moti Mama? Why not Raqib? What was the point of this collective treachery? Apparently, my mother got unexpectedly delayed in her errands. Moti Mama thought I needed the sleep and kept Raqib from calling me. Raqib went away after a short and desultory practice by himself. The sheer unthinking apathy of this crew filled me with fury.

When I confronted them, Moti Mama offered to go play with me in the dark. We stood in the living room, and I could see the front lawn brimming with darkness as if poured out of a giant vat above. My mother promised to let me play an extra hour the next day. But, you can't give me back this afternoon! I screamed. No hour later can be a substitute for the hour that is gone! They stared at me with uncomprehending but sympathetic smiles.

I railed at my mother and at Moti Mama until I broke down into inconsolable sobs. What's gone is gone! Didn't they understand? I kicked the ball with all the frustrated rage of my seven-year-old body, and watched it fly out through the open living-room door into the barely visible lawn. Having had enough of my tantrum, my mother sent me back to my room and threatened no TV that night if I didn't stop. As if television mattered! As if anything else mattered!

With slow and heavy steps I came back to my unlit room and, in place of the fury over the lost game, what emerged slowly was an element of wonder that anything could be lost irretrievably. I could suddenly see the fragility and the deception of our routines. They created a sense of recurrence where all that existed was a vanishing presence. I did not possess the vocabulary then for everything that I understood nonetheless. I realized that there were forces out there from which even my mother could not protect me. No longer angry, I felt sorry for her, and for myself. And that was how, robbed of a winter's afternoon, I first came to learn what was sorrow.

I don't know if everyone experiences a moment like the one I did as a seven-year-old. Perhaps everyone does, but at an older age. Perhaps some people never do. What I do know, however, is that much of our lives as adults, which is what I am now and have been for many years, are about creating defenses against such precarious moments. Our happiness, indeed sanity itself, depends on the quality of one's parapets. I felt fairly well served by mine, until last Tuesday, when I visited Ibid. I liked the store, because it alone in this town boasted a philosophy section of any richness, and offered the added advantage of being located close to my office. A little staircase led up to the lofted section where the philosophers rubbed shoulders in an erratic jumble. For unknown reasons,

Germans dominated the shelves. Dusty old copies of Schopenhauer and Hegel jostled with Nietzsche and Heidegger. I would pull down a volume at random and sit down on the little bench against the trellised iron railing. The murmur of housewives gossiping around the center display below was muffled by a noisy, dripping air-conditioner. I started reading wherever my eyes fell, sometimes for an hour, at times longer. The staff knew me well, and let me be. It did not matter where I picked up my reading, the conversations felt familiar and repetitive. The magnificent irrelevancy of these distant white men was oddly soothing to my unhinged soul.

I could not talk to anyone in Dhaka. Intellectual curiosity for men in this city ran as far as the latest car model or electronic gadget. At best one talked of politics or the mergers of big businesses. Best airport lounges of the world, or new restaurants in town. The women were no better; only the objects of their fascination differed. When we talk to someone we plunge into another consciousness, and if we are lucky it offers some depth. There will be sudden bends in the stream, an unexpected eddy somewhere, the gift of surprise, if not recognition. I longed for the depth of streams, rivers, perhaps the sea, but my interlocutors landed me again and again in dirty street puddles. So I had stopped looking for an answer in other people. In the years after my parting with Ayesha, for some time I thought a perfect connection could be found again with patience, with searching. The twenty-five years since our last meeting has taught me otherwise. I have learned that our metaphysical needs can be met only by chance.

As an adult, I have devoted my energies to solving life's practical problems, and I can't say I have done too badly. I live alone in a lovely apartment—in Banani again, after all these years—and have built up my own ad agency. It isn't the biggest agency in town, but it lets me live in sufficient style and we do interesting work. I take two vacations a year, often to exotic locales. Last year, Ireland and Mauritius. What I enjoy most, however, are my little daily freedoms, like my trips to Ibid. When I entered Ibid last Tuesday, I exchanged conspiratorial glances with the manager, a long-toothed and yolk-eyed ancient whom I suspected of being the subversive cause behind the German bias of the philosophy shelves. The store seemed more crowded than usual, but my little perch was mercifully free of any intruders. Even the small walk from my office left me hot and sweaty, and I was thankful that the AC, noisier than usual, was operating. With luck there would be no power outage, not till I cooled down.

I scanned the shelves, and pulled down a worn out copy of *Beyond Good and Evil*. Of all Nietzsche's works, this was my favorite. I liked the direct yet anguished attacks not just on ideas but also on their hapless bearers. Here was a man whose rage I could relate to, though I had no desire to share his troubles in exact details–syphilis, madness, and early death. Poor man, how tormented he was! I loved the visceral intensity of his expressions, the urgency. *Philosophers should indeed be, as he says, investigators to the point of cruelty, with rash fingers for the ungraspable, with teeth and stomach for the most indigestible.* When I was a young man I thought I might become a philosopher, or at least a writer. While in reality I have gotten no closer to writing anything but the copy, with which I sustain my lonely altitude, I think in fundamental disposition I've come closer to living like a writer than the frauds who claim that identity with annual publications. They're no better than the philosophers who so riled Nietzsche. *What's attractive about looking at all philosophers in part suspiciously and in part mockingly is not that... they make mistakes and get lost...but that they are not honest enough... they defend with reasons sought out after the fact of...an idea, an "inspiration"...*It had been a long time since I'd last come across these passages, and they swept over me with the gratifying sonority of an almost forgotten but beloved old song. I pushed the bench up against the end of one shelf so I could lean back. This was what I did if I fell into pages worthy of immersion.

I could tell, from a familiarity with the pattern of his sorties, that he was winding up for a fresh assault on his nemeses. But before I could sink into the next section, suddenly the power went out. There was a lot less light outside, and very little of it penetrated the deck where I was sitting. I closed the book on my lap and waited for a staff member to bring up a halogen lamp.

The store manager sauntered, with his lopsided walk, up to the front door to guard against shoplifters. Most of the shoppers were hidden in their aisles. I could only see three women, standing in a tiny triangle. One of them I could see only from the back, and another's face was obscured by the brim of a stylish head-scarf. The third, who caught my attention, was a short-haired woman in a burgundy sari. I could see only a side of her face, and yet, with a strange dislocation within myself, I knew it was Ayesha. Despite the changes wrought by time, in her case quite subtle, the way she stood—leaning heavily on one foot—and the tilt of the head, the skin, dark as molasses, it was all quite unmistakable. As if sensing my stare, she looked up in my direction. My first instinct, even though I had anticipated this precise moment for years, was to pull back, and sometimes that's all it takes—the tiniest flutter of a hesitation. By the time I looked again, seconds later, she was gone.

I climbed downstairs, and found that all three women had disappeared. I did not even know if they were together. I asked the manager if he knew them. "No sir, not regulars," he said, with a wobble of his head. I stood around dumbly in the store for a few more moments, as if Ayesha, if it were indeed her, would wander back inside.

The Ibid's street was packed with stores, cafes, offices, and the consequent crush of people and cars. There was no hope of finding anyone who merged into this crowd. Still I came outside and looked right and left. Our circles did not overlap at all, and I had received only intermittent reports about her over the years from Raqib, who, like some people, had grown less reliable with age. Only the basic facts could be trusted: Ayesha was married with two kids, and she had moved back to Dhaka after many years abroad. Finding her would not be too difficult, if I really wanted to do so. But I had left any meeting to chance, all these years, in the hope—apparently vain—that chance might suffice where courage had failed.

To tell the story of Ayesha, I have to go back to the time we moved from Banani to Uttara. A relocation to a new and usually cheaper neighborhood was the result of my father's troubled career. Having made GM in an insurance company a few years back, he was now sliding laterally to smaller and less reputable companies. I hated the somber evenings when we would sit around the dining table while my father enumerated what was wrong with his new job. Each venture started with an injection of optimism. Then one day he'd report how his new boss lost his temper, in front of outsiders! "A British manager would have known to call a man into his room," my father would say, ruefully shaking his head at the world's plummeting civility. By the time the stories culminated in hints of an office-wide conspiracy, I knew we weren't far from another firing. I wished there was something I could do to protect him, but I also resented the impending move.

When we first shifted to Uttara, the city authorities were still busy carving up plots in the newer sections. The horizon was much wider there – and farther away – than anywhere else in Dhaka. The edges of the neighborhood gave away to clumps of trees, paddy fields, and scattered hutments. New owners ogled the rise of their stunted manors, while workers hung dangerously off of bamboo scaffoldings.

Even as Dhaka expanded, many lives were getting smaller. The prospect of becoming trapped in one of those small lives filled me with terror. Surely, there had to be another world, another kind of life, one that would be full of amplitude, even elegance! A determination to find that world took root within me like an irritating pebble that can't be dislodged from inside a shoe.

Around this time I started spending all my time at Raqib's. He was still my best friend, my only real friend. They still lived in Banani. We were in the final year of college. After classes we ambled over to his place, and listened to his music collection, which ranged from Western pop-trash to obscure ghazals. Music had replaced football as his chief passion. I'd discovered books. But, I didn't mind the music. No matter how loudly Raqib played it, I found a good book blotted out the world.

I'd be on the sofa reading a book, while Raqib drew endless designs on the floor with his finger, waiting to flip the cassette.

I liked his parents. His father came from work bearing gifts or stories, or took us all out for a drive, without occasion, to go eat shish kebab from his favorite road-side shop. What I liked better however was his mother's cooking. Often I stayed for dinner. Be it a simple chicken curry or elaborate mughlai parathas, her entire oeuvre I found addictive. Or perhaps it wasn't the cooking, but their household that absorbed me. It was a happier place to be. They seemed to live in a house with all the lights turned on. Whereas ours...the only light in it, my mother, and even her bravery was starting to falter as the cycles of my father's dysfunction quickened.

Raqib talked of going abroad. Of finding the right girl. Or, for now, any girl. He just wanted to have sex first.

"C'mon, think about it, what if you got run over tomorrow? Do you really want to die a virgin?"

Once, a terrible thought occurred to me: Your life is so perfect, if one of us were indeed to die young, it'd probably be you! But I didn't tell him that, at least not that day. I went back to my book without any replies, and he went on about the girl who'd moved in next door. The girl of course was Ayesha. No sooner had he received news of this girl who possessed three vital qualities—a girl, our age, and right next door— then Raqib dutifully went up to the roof to conduct a ritual inspection. According to him, she possessed three further virtues—a shapely figure, visual availability, and a fairly dependable schedule—which clearly invited a sustained watch. But I refused to participate in these furtive vigils.

"What the fuck's wrong with you, man? How else are you going to see her?" Raqib challenged me.

"Don't worry. It'll happen if it's meant to be." I said, knowing full well the anguish my apathetic response would provoke in him.

"Meant to be? It's been two weeks already!"

"Two weeks is not that long. You have to trust destiny," I said, still complacent.

"Fuck your destiny, man. This isn't going anywhere," said Raqib.

"And trawling on the roof is doing wonders for you, you dimwit?"

We went back and forth like that. Raqib stuck to his methods and brought back details that he felt were important. Today she sported a purple head-band. Today she was accompanied by an angry-looking aunt. Today she wore a sleeveless silk shirt. I could not explain to Raqib why nothing could move me to take part in this escapade. Every day at five, the roofs of Dhaka filled with young men like us, and even girls like Ayesha, longing to see or be seen. A few of them probably even established contact, developed romance, or at least friendships. But I wanted no part of it. I suspected Ayesha didn't either. If Raqib's reports were correct, she came up mainly to watch over her younger brother as he flew his kites.

As I saw it: Raqib would someday go abroad. Raqib would find other forms of exaltation in life. My destiny seemed far more uncertain. I felt no desire to add the taint of roof-top courtships to all the other ways in which the city had already demoted me.

Days passed. Raqib disapproved of me openly. Then one Saturday morning, as I was walking up to Raqib's—I always walked from the bus-stop—I saw Ayesha, in red track pants, on the road with a bicycle. Girls our age didn't ride bikes often. This took me by surprise. She stopped at her gate, leaning on one foot, probably deciding if she should go inside or keep riding.

I noticed Raqib, from the corner of my eye, on his roof. In a spasm of wicked wit, I decided to approach Ayesha, not that we knew her name yet. Without ever glancing up at Raqib, I walked straight over straight to Ayesha and introduced myself. I told her I kind of lived there, next door to her. She did not brush me off, as any girl should a stranger who approaches her on the street. We talked, standing at her gate, and what was meant to be a passing encounter turned into a full-fledged conversation.

She told me that her family had just moved back from London. That she went to an English medium school, not too far away. It came out that we were the same year in school, though she struck me as somehow younger. She did most of the talking. She did not ask me at any point to come inside, but she also showed no impatience to bring our road-side chat to a conclusion. She told me that she didn't have many friends yet, and that she felt a little disturbed by the kind of stares she got on the streets.

"It must be difficult for you," I said. "I'm sorry we didn't come by sooner to say hello."

"That's all right," she said. "I could have come over too."

Clearly, she was from another world. She didn't know that we were meant to exist on opposite sides of an invisible yet impenetrable curtain; that by talking to me she was conferring a form of favor on me, the kind not easily granted by local girls. They were terrified of being judged, of conferring any favor on an unworthy candidate. Any girl who was this unaware of local protocols could just as well be a foreigner.

By the time I came up to Raqib's, the poor chap was on the verge of committing suicide. "That's it, you just went up to her and said hello? What the fuck man? What the fuck? I thought you weren't even interested in her. I thought you were becoming a homo!"

He could call me whatever he wanted. I had not felt so good in a long time. I just didn't care. No matter how much he taunted or cajoled me, trying to pry out the contents of my talks with Ayesha, I refused to yield any details.

"So you just walk up to a girl, and talk to her? And it's fine?"

Yes, but if you did it, I thought, you'd probably get slapped. And this time, I told him what I thought.

Even Raqib had to laugh. He threw the cassette-tape in his hand at my head and with enough force to crack it on the wall when I ducked. He shook his head and cast me a dismayed look, as if to say, how is this possible, how could you end up talking to her?

"Fucking destiny," I said, still laughing.

My affair with Ayesha occurred so long ago, and we were so young. Yet Ayesha is still the girl that I dream of most often. I wake up in the middle of the night, trying to complete conversations left open at the time of our parting. Reprising evening walks around Banani Lake, her scent–thick as mud, sweet as jasmine–pierces me as if she'd just left the room.

Ayesha lived in a classic two-story Banani house, surrounded by mature trees. A beautiful lawn adorned the front, where her parents took tea, when her father wasn't on one of his frequent trips. When I visited her, I felt as if I had walked into an advertisement. I expected someone to order me off the set at any moment. I was introduced to her parents, with some element of truth, as the boy from next door.

Ayesha and I spent a great deal of time, ironically, on the roof. We didn't go there by choice, but we were sent there to chaperone her brother who loved flying kites. I thought of kites as a village sport and could not fathom how a boy from London could become so enamored of it. As it turned out, Numair was not the only aficionado. A kite fad seemed to have infected the neighborhood, and a spirited boy like Numair was easily drawn to the thrill of kite-fights. As his kites soared to new heights, even we could not help but be mesmerized by their ersatz shapes and colors. And the beauty of their flight-paths: long and sinewy at times, skittish and troubled at others. What brilliantly colored kites he flew! They were mostly bought for him by his father, on his trips abroad, whereas others Numair claimed to have constructed himself.

"Well, not entirely by himself," Ayesha would tell me with a wink.

Up until I met Ayesha, I had no specific expectation as to when or how a girl might come into my life. Even at that young age I doubted there was any such thing as true love, or one true love. I didn't doubt that there was love, and that even my seemingly fortressed existence would be exposed to that phenomenon someday. But I didn't recognize Ayesha right away as the inception of that event. There was no reason to in the first few months, when we treated each other more like friends.

I could talk to Ayesha like I could with no one else. I talked to her about my father. What a sad and pathetic case he was. How his predicament filled me with worry. Will we fall farther yet? What dead-end job will he take up next? Where will we move to then? I talked about the house in Banani where we grew up. And the joy and certitude that filled our lives in those days. My father was a different man then. More than anything, I told her, it terrified me that I too might turn out to be like my father.

"No, no, that won't happen," Ayesha would say as she shook her head, and the ends of her short hair lightly flicked her cheeks.

"How do you know?" I'd insist.

"I know," she said. "I can tell. You won't be like him. Or like anyone else. You will be different."

Ayesha's appraisal filled me with a kind of confidence I'd never known till then. Until then I felt I existed, like everyone else, for no particular reason, but simply because I'd suffered the biological accident of birth. I was already an atheist. I read Sartre. I read Camus. I also read Asimov and Conan Doyle. And a retinue of Bengali sentimentalists. But what I read didn't matter. That I expected someone to give me an answer was the point. It sure wasn't coming from my father, or from my teachers, or any other grown-up I knew. I wanted to reach the place, not just the physical terrain, where all the writers lived. These were things I could tell Ayesha. She didn't dismiss me as pretentious, or a fool. She seemed to think what I said made sense. And she displayed infinite patience for the endless unspooling of my ideas and speculations, their revisions and re-visitations. Until I met her, I didn't even know that I possessed the need for someone like her. Ideas – and anguish – inchoate till then due to lack of expression, were finally aspirated – and validated. With them, I too was becoming valid.

Ayesha was contemplative in a deeply concealed manner. "We can really only know what's in our mind, isn't it? So maybe we're friends not 'cause we understand each other," she said to me– sitting on top of the water-tank on their roof one evening– "but because we misunderstand each other perfectly." She made her pronouncements spontaneously and as if they hardly mattered.

In the parcel of contradictions that was Ayesha, I was only one element. I could tell that her other friends didn't like me at all. They didn't trust me. I didn't quite belong to their sphere, and they were right. Only Ayesha couldn't see it. Or, she didn't care. But then she didn't exactly belong to their orbit either, or to any orbit for that matter.

She shared greater surface resemblance with these friends than she did with me: rich kids who lived in Gulshan or Banani and went to English medium schools. She dressed like them, and at other times like trampy Londoners, in tight black jeans and with black eyeliner. The first winter after we'd met, she dyed streaks of purple into her hair and nearly got herself expelled from school. I could tell that she intimidated both the boys and the girls in her group, which is why they didn't protest too much when she brought a misfit like me along.

The most regular excursions of her group centered on Video Mania, where weekend visits were mandatory for anyone who remotely aspired to coolness. In a town where everything was prohibited, the place became a destination of sorts. It was much bigger than any normal store, plushly carpeted and mirrored, and pumping trendy, hot music. Idiots like Ayesha's friends went there dressed as if they were going to a club. To my dismay, and some annoyance, Ayesha too would want to go there.

"Really, Video Mania? We have to go there?"

"Yes, what else is there to do?" Ayesha would say on Saturday evenings, when she dragged me there in my defiantly plain shirts and faded jeans.

Afterwards we'd hop over to the burger joint right next door. This place too was jazzed up to feel like something more than what it was, with sinfully named innocent drinks and karaoke loaded with the hippest releases from around the world. To sit there with Ayesha's friends, while they sang in their put-on accents, was pure torture for me. But, of course that's where we found ourselves on New Year's Eve.

"Don't be so glum all the time," Ayesha said to me. We were sitting in a booth watching her friend Arshad make an ass of himself with the microphone. Everyone was supposed to go over to his place at ten; this was just the warm up party.

"You know I don't like this scene," I said.

"Why, what's so wrong with it?"

"What's not wrong with it? Where do I even start?"

"Don't start," said Ayesha, cutting me off like she'd never done before. "It's a perfectly fine place, everyone's having a good time. Must you philosophize everything into meaninglessness?"

"Actually, in this case I don't even have to philosophize," I said.

"Don't be such a snob, don't look down on everything all the time," said Ayesha.

"That's what I do? Is that what you think?"

"I don't think that, my dear. I know it, I see it," she said, softening the criticism with a smile.

I knew she was right, but I had never been criticized by her before. I went quiet, digesting the import of what she said. If I were such a repository of gloom and aloofness, why did she hang out with me?

"Now, don't get all sulky on me. Come, sing with me," she said, as she stood up. She tried to pull me up, but I wouldn't budge. Her friends started looking at us.

"C'mon now, don't be so stubborn," she said, still holding my hand.

"You go ahead, you know I can't sing," I said sullenly.

Suddenly she dropped my hand, turned around and walked over to the microphone. I could feel a roomful of stares on me, silently saying, what an asshole! I sat there for some time, still unable to go up and join her. If I'd got up, within seconds of her turning around, the moment could have been salvaged.

I stayed for some more time and watched her sing with Arshad. The strobe lights gave me a headache, and Ayesha's fractured image in that flashing light made her seem more distant. She sang with big, fat, fair, happy, oblivious Arshad, and anyone looking at them would have thought they were best friends, or even an item.

The way she could seem to belong to whomever she was with at a given moment bothered me. I was sure that the Ayesha who hung out with me was the real one, but then when I saw other versions of her, they seemed so authentic, I lost my sense of surety. And specialness.

On that night, it upset me more than I could understand, provoking a feeling akin to jealousy, even though I knew there was nothing between her and Arshad, or any other boy for that matter. But, suddenly it mattered to me that there should be nothing between her and anyone else, at least nothing that compared or competed with whatever was there between us. But what was that? Until then it had no name, nor acknowledgment, not even in the privacy of our minds, as far as I could tell.

Ayesha was possibly the best singer in her group. So, when she took the microphone, she could keep it virtually as long as she wanted. When Arshad came away, someone else, another boy or girl, went and joined her. Even other people in the joint, total strangers, didn't object to her monopoly of the microphone, but happily joined her when their turn came up. As long as I was there, she didn't look at me again. Well before it was time to remove to Arshad's, I left the place without saying goodbye to Ayesha or anyone else.

I'd be lying if I said that I hadn't imagined Ayesha as something more than a friend. I certainly found her physically attractive. And I'd begun to find many of her manners adorable–rotating her bangles when inventing innocent lies for her mother or slicing her food always through the tines of her fork. Until New Year's, I had felt she was somehow mine, even though there was no such commitment between us. I had thought I'd have all the time in the world to establish my claim. Sensing my assumptions to be delusional, I was suddenly in panic.

"I told you, too much talking. Always talking. And some bugger's going to just come and whisk her away." This was Raqib's assessment of the situation. Raqib, who was yet to manage a morsel of a conversation with a decent girl, was my advisor.

"You have to do something, man. You've got to tell her. Here's what you do, you get her flowers. No, let me make a tape for you. Take the flowers, and the tape. And leave them with a letter. I'll help you write it. It has to be on scented paper. I know where to get it." Raqib never lacked for enthusiasm. But, as much as I appreciated the merit of his basic observations, I wasn't about to let him conduct a romance vicariously through me.

It had been almost two weeks since New Year's, and I hadn't seen Ayesha since that night. She had not called me either—not that she did that often anyway. We hardly ever called each other on the telephone. She knew and respected my pathological aversion for that instrument. But for a person as forthright as Ayesha, allowing such a hiatus was unusual. It seemed significant, but what was the significance? A few rounds of analysis with Raqib led to depressing and disturbing possibilities, so I'd stopped talking even with him. Unable to withstand the suspense, or go any longer without seeing her, I went over to her place again one morning.

Their driver opened the gate for me. I didn't need anyone to lead me in. When I entered the living room, I found Ayesha lying sideways on the sofa, in a velvet sweater, with the fourth book from the Malory Towers series clutched close to her chest. I knew what it meant for her to be curled up with this childhood favorite. This was where she went when she felt tired or small. She'd made me read the entire series right before New Year's. She said I couldn't understand her if I didn't know the characters. When I finished the series and asked who she was in the book, quite typically she said she could be any of them—Darrell or Alicia or Sally, even Mary-Lou or Irene, but never Gwendolyn or Bill. It depended on the day, she said.

"So, who are we today?" I asked, as I sat down on the sofa near her feet.

Ayesha sat up, but didn't say anything. A gauzy white curtain billowed softly in the breeze that came through the open window. She continued reading her book, not in a manner that seemed to say, you are not welcome here, but rather to say that I could be part of the comforts that these books provided her. I was happy just to be sitting there with her, watching the white winter light play inside the hesitant swells of the curtain.

"You are such an odd boy," she said, when she finally closed her book and spoke to me.

"I don't try to be odd," I began to explain, and she gave a gentle laugh.

I knew we were becoming more than friends, but I did not seek immediate confirmation. I was once again willing to take time, and let chance play its part. My patience, or rather seeming passivity, drove Raqib to a fit of condemnation: you gutless little git! You don't deserve her! You don't deserve any girl, or anything! You should just get run over and be done with your miseries. Poor Raqib was quite frustrated by this time with his lack of progress on the romantic front. But I wasn't miserable at all. For the first time in my life I was actually feeling content, even elated, mainly due to an indefinable note of intimacy that had entered my interactions with Ayesha.

When she looked at me now, it was with a kind of warmth that I hadn't seen before. And for the moment, that was all the confirmation I needed. She gave me a Matchbox set of beautiful old cars—including a model of a green MG Midget—for my birthday, and said, "Someday, I'll get you a real one."

"And, maybe by then I'll learn to drive," I said.

"You don't have to. You can just have the car," she replied.

A week later, when we were climbing up the stairs to the roof, I touched her lightly on the shoulder. She stopped, turned—and before I could make another move—she kissed me with a strong, moist, pressure of her lips, and then resumed climbing with the statement, "You are an idiot. Only you would wait for so long."

The period that followed was one of unnerving bliss. My National Board Exams were a month away that spring. I found it hard to concentrate on my studies. I had only Ayesha on my mind. I'd pack my books and tell my mother I was going over to study with Raqib. She held me with the same tenebrous gaze that she reserved for my father and his tales. I could not ignore that gaze, not entirely. While I'd learned a long time ago that she could not protect me, I had not yet renounced a reciprocal obligation towards her. So, I studied late into the nights, but my days were consumed by Ayesha.

I never minded watching Numair fly his kites on their roof, but now I suddenly found even the sillier obligations of being with Ayesha–getting ice-cream at Candy Floss, or jaunts to Video Mania–much less stressful. When you're nineteen, it's amazing what the advent of physical intimacy will do to improve your tolerance for the world and its inhabitants. I could listen to my father with greater sympathy. I could laugh with Arshad. Somehow the certainty of knowing that the Ayesha whom I knew, not just in our talks, but the one I now got to hold in my arms, was the real one, and mine, made me feel deeply content and powerful.

After the exams, I was without occupation. The entrance exams for the local universities were still far away, not till winter. I had never been so free. I decided to start living like a writer. I read till late into the night, and sometimes wrote long, frenzied–what I imagined were inspired–speculations about the nature of things, reality, consciousness. I myself found them quite unintelligible at times if I read them again at a space of few weeks, or even days, but I was undeterred in the composition of my nocturnes. When the writing did not flow, I read or translated passages from a kindred source. I woke up late in the mornings to my mother's deep but increasingly resigned disapproval.

My days were of course still occupied fully with Ayesha. I could spend hours unfurling the ideas that colonized my nights. Ayesha would listen patiently, while fixing her brother's kites or her father's Technics turntable. She was always doing something. One day I'd come to her house and find her in the kitchen, covered in baking powder. Another day, she'd be with her bike, disassembled on the lawn, fingers black with lubricant oil. She'd take out their second car, a green Datsun—a bit of a relic by then—for a spin when her father wasn't in town. Her mother's mild protestations were no match for Ayesha's verve and confidence.

On one of these long and illicit drives, she suggested to me that my problem wasn't Dhaka, but my nature. Some people are born to be content, presumably like her, and could make a happy enough life with whatever crooked and partial materials life threw at them. Whereas others like me, perhaps a minority, were born with the ability to conceive of alternatives, and the cursed inclination to imagine them to be better.

As it happened, she was right. We had been together for a few months, and each stage of increased intimacy was thrilling, momentarily scary, but ultimately a revelation. Just few months before, I expected not even a soft look from a girl. But sometimes the utter lack of a possibility is better. The partial availability of the object only serves to ignite and expand the need. Besides, there was my reliable goad, Raqib, to stoke any discontents, especially on this front.

"Really, man, no breakthrough yet? Not once?" Raqib asked me.

"No, she's quite shy about these things," I said.

Frankly, I too was surprised by Ayesha's reserve. At first I thought it was mainly because she did not want to risk getting caught *in flagrante*. Finding adequate privacy was often a challenge. We could hang out as much as we wanted—in their living room, or on the roof. But we weren't allowed to go to her bedroom. I obviously never invited her to my place. So while we had all the time for long, lingering kisses, the act was always crimped by the possibility of someone—her mother, or a maid—walking in on us. In passing, it also occurred to me that perhaps I was not her first. That our kisses, the palpitating anticipation of the next meeting, all this was not as new to her as they were to me. But I knew better than to let this dismal thought develop too much.

"I thought foreign girls were supposed to be easy," Raqib said to me.

"She's not exactly foreign, you know. She only lived there for a few years," I said.

"Who're you kidding, man? We both know she's basically foreign, and she won't give it to you. You think someone her age, living there, doesn't have experience?"

"Watch it, Raqib. You're talking about my girlfriend," I'd say, losing my usual detachment.

Raqib was full of disdain for my situation. He had recently visited a prostitute, because it was just time to be "done with the thing." He felt in no way ashamed or degraded by the experience. Rather, he felt lighter now that the suspense was over, and even held that bit of carnal knowledge as an attainment over me. It didn't matter that he'd paid for it, and that there was no love involved. He knew what a woman looked like, and I didn't. It was hard to argue with such blunt simplicities, but I felt no need to convince him. The pace of my affair was perfectly fine, as far as I was concerned. There was no need to get greedy.

"Yeah, tell yourself that," said Raqib, shooting a tennis ball into the hoop he'd set up against one wall.

"You don't understand anything. You can't rush these things. They have their own tempo," I told him.

I was spending more time with Raqib, because Ayesha was visiting universities in London with her father. She'd done very well in her "A" levels, and it was always understood that she'd go to London for her studies. That eventuality posed questions that neither of us seemed ready to address. They filled me with foreboding at times, and made me want to start detaching myself from Ayesha. Why prolong—let alone deepen—something that was, in any event, headed for dissolution?

Looking back, I am amazed at how much patience I possessed at that age. I realize now I have been growing up in reverse. I was gentle and understanding with Ayesha, the way one might be with an interlude much later in life, when one has vast experience and little expectation. But all my affairs since then have been mainly a chronicle of misdemeanors. I am unable to conduct myself with women in a manner that doesn't lead to their throwing things at me. Flowers, shoes, vases, once even a portable heater. What have they not inflicted on me, and more importantly – I'd be the first to admit it – what have I not visited upon them? My deficiencies as an adult can't all be blamed on my thwarted affair with Ayesha. Life's not like that. Nothing scars us or shapes us permanently. We simply emerge to be the selves we were destined to be and seek out causal links to events and people in the past that we think provide an answer. Be that as it may, by now I'm fully grown into my malfunctions. I go for months without initiating anything with a woman. After Ayesha, I didn't date anyone for seven years. During the purgative stretches I retreat to Ibid or my own study; adrift in the continent of my words. It's a beautiful place: vast, arid, and most crucially, free of people. If I could physically manifest that domain, it'd smell of gusty dry desert wind. But I can't remain there forever. There are other corners of the terrain, full of other compulsions, that also exercise a hold on me. I don't mean just the sexual impulse, which is an undeniable force, but even more the allure of hope itself–a recurrent expectation that one of these encounters will prove to be different and bring a greater measure of completion to my life, or myself, without requiring me to change in any crucial manner.

So, I meet a new woman and maybe she reminds me of Ayesha, or she's alluring because she's like no one else I've known before. A mix of perfume and self-delusion, the right music over an adequately exotic dinner, builds up to an attraction that feels genuine. And new quirks of personality, a moment of passing perfection get added to the memories. One woman insisted on walking everywhere, another would make me drive her even to Ibid. I recall women who were generous in bed, contemplative in bed, full of demands or peculiar reservations; women who sighed too much, or screamed too loud; women with whom I was happy to take long walks, or visit second-hand markets, until it was time to part because one always reaches that point. The only one to whom I ever proposed–and later withdrew, a ghastly scene–was a compulsive folder and filer: sheets, towels, clothes, napkins in restaurants, papers in doctor's waiting rooms. I myself am a big believer of order, but her I had to let go (for other reasons). I am always surprised by what the mind remembers; as if the particles gathered from all the different encounters would add up to a totality. I see the falsity of such expectations, and wish to withdraw, but every modality poses its own set of risks. There are women who become drawn to me simply because I seem aloof, unavailable. And these are not just young, impressionable ones. Mostly I can find a gentle way to rebuff the innocents. Sometimes it leads to a lachrymose evening and promises of an attenuated friendship. But there are others, the experienced ones, who should know better. Yet even they succumb—as do I. Don't get me wrong. I don't mean to present myself as an accomplished seducer. Plenty of men, even women, have had many more partners than I ever will. My only goal is to find a way to engage women without raising any obligations. Before I ever bring them back to my place, I make it amply clear that any relationship with me can go only so far. "Don't worry, I understand," they say. "I'm not looking for anything serious either." Long past the rituals, I get up in the middle of the night to fetch a glass of water, and I see the woman lost inside the foamy gathering of my silky blue sheets, and depending on the night, and the point in the engagement, I am filled with pity or sorrow or self-disgust.

If I knew then everything that I know now, I would have dissolved my relations with Ayesha long before it actually ended. As it happened, I went to see Ayesha the day she came back from London. It had been a month, and she looked different. She was sitting in their living room in a burgundy colored T-shirt, tighter than usual. A plethora of gifts lay strewn on the white sofa. I didn't care about the gifts, not even the books. I was instantly and desperately in love again from the moment I saw her. I refused to leave her alone; the only proof I wanted of her love was in her acceding to my relentless demands. I cornered her in the living room, in passageways. I dropped my caution even in places—the empty kitchen, the parked car—previously thought to be too unsafe.

"What's gotten into you?" she asked laughing, not entirely displeased.

The realization that she'd be gone in a few months terrified me. I could not bear the thought of being in Dhaka without her, but I also could not see any real possibility for me to leave. I knew that culminating our affair in a physical sense offered no answer to the brute divergence in our paths; rather any deepening of intimacy might only make the inevitable separation harder. Ayesha however was still sanguine. She did not see the separation as inevitable. "You know there are scholarships one can get," she said. She blamed me for not even exploring the possibility, for not trying. This led to a big fight, and once again we spent New Year's apart.

When we made up, we also finally had sex. So, our first sex was make-up sex. It was a hurried and awkward affair, in her living room. It's hard to lose yourself completely, if you have to keep your ears open for footsteps or the rustle of a curtain. After that day I became newly obsessed with her. The manic pull of the physical experience itself was intense. How she smelled, how she felt under my touch, every motion or gesture, got replayed in my mind until there was a chance to register a new and surprising set of notations. She, who was so reticent until then, seemed equally intoxicated by the newness and rawness of the experience. Once the initial barrier was crossed, she never resisted me again. But even this unbridled acceptance brought no lasting solace for me. Every time I saw her, even when we were apart, I could never forget one thing–: she's leaving, she's leaving. The thought fluttered inside my skull like a bird desperate to get out of a room. No matter how many times I kissed her, where I kissed her, how I held her, how long or deeply I looked into her eyes, there was no arresting the inexorable movement of time. The happiest moments were marked by an undertone of panic and sadness. And the feelings were heightened by the fact that they were not shared equally by Ayesha. She clung to the belief that we'd somehow continue even after she left. Neither of us pressed the point too much;

it led to tears or acrimony. I did not want any discord during this period, when time was short, and felt shorter with each passing day.

By late spring, I could almost count the days left to us, not that I actually counted them. That would be too depressing. I was afraid she'd meet someone in London, and I'd be evicted from this improbable respite back to the dreary smallness of Dhaka. Certain days I deliberately refrained from coming to see Ayesha. I wanted to see what it'd be like to live without her. I could not stay home, and I could not even go to Raqib's–it was too close to her place. I'd spend a day browsing the bookstores in New Market. I walked aimlessly through the streets of Dhaka. And then, pulled by a force greater than my will, I ended up still at her house at odd times.

"Don't be so sad all the time, please," said Ayesha.

"You'll go to a new place, meet new people, it's easier for you," I said.

"Don't say it like that. It's not like I mean to leave you. And I know you don't want to hear it now, but maybe after I leave you'll see, you'll find a way to come over," she insisted.

Our conversations, which once gave me an immense sense of relief, were now stuck on a point. We were safe when we could talk about other things, but how long could we avoid talking about London? And how fair would that be to Ayesha? Even I enjoyed hearing about her university, where it was located, who else was going there. I had always enjoyed dreaming of other places. I just didn't like what London meant for us now.

It was May, and we were sitting on the water-tank on Ayesha's roof. It had rained that morning and again briefly right before, in the afternoon, before we came up. Numair was pulling back a black kite after a short flight. Apparently, something was not quite right with its shape or size for the kind of wind that was available. We didn't mind getting the backs of our jeans wet. I was actually leaning back on my elbows, so even my shirt was getting splotchy with water-stains. It was nice to sit up in the coolness after a shower.

"You know, the rain in London won't smell like this," I said.

"How do you know? You've never even been there," she said.

"No, but I can see it clearly. It's my gift, don't you know? I can tell what other places and other times are like without having to visit them in person."

"Is that so?" she laughed.

"Yes, right now I can just see you in London. Walking in the miserable, stingy drizzle they call rain. You've forgotten your umbrella and you're all wet. You're trying to find cover under an awning. You wish you were home, with me," I said.

"Is that how it'll be, my clairvoyant?" Ayesha said, turning to caress my face with an open palm. Earlier when we were in the living room, we were interrupted by her mother, who thought to bring us some freshly baked cake. But a touch from her now, suddenly rekindled a feeling in me. She could see it in my eyes, and smiled a "no" at me with a silent gesture towards her brother. Numair was about to start unfurling his big yellow kite.

I was not easily dissuaded once the notion entered my head. I sat up a little and tugged at the back of Ayesha's shirt. She brushed my hand away, but not in a manner that conveyed conviction. I was so avaricious in those last days, as if I wanted to swallow her in bits and pieces. As if, each time we made love, I was absorbing a bit more of her to store away, and the stock of memories and sensations thus gathered would keep me whole even after she was gone.

She knew how insistent I could be. Ayesha slipped down from the water-tank, and cast a glance at the most private corner of the roof. It would not be the first time we'd sneaked off to that corner to make out. It was against one wall of the stairwell. Two of the open sides were covered by big trees. The final side was obstructed by the water-tank, which meant Numair would not run over to that part all of a sudden.

I pressed her against the wall, and inhaled a sweet, keen floral scent rising whether from her hair or her skin, I never knew. In that instant there was no London, no time, no decisions or choices. Beneath the light summery cloth of her blouse, her skin felt taut and alert. I brushed my hand slowly down her exposed arm, until it came to rest on her hip. Then I started kissing her. She kept her eyes closed, and seemed more acquiescent than usual. There was no sense of hurry in her. We had never gone all the way on the roof. Not with someone else pattering about in another corner of it. But as I reached the cold steel button of her jeans, she did not protest. Really, here? Now? I wasn't about to question either her judgment or my luck. And I wasn't sure even that this was what she meant, but she placed a hand against my nape, and deepened the kiss.

At that precise moment, we heard a sharp, sudden cry from the other end of the roof. Even before we'd seen anything, from the uncanny high pitch of the cry and its abrupt end, I knew Numair had fallen. We swung around from our corner in an instant, but did not see Numair anywhere on the roof. Ayesha called out his name, with an eerie quaver in her voice—wishing to hold the world still with her voice—as she rushed to the edge of the roof. I spotted the yellow kite stuck on a jack-fruit tree, and I knew exactly what had happened. He'd seen me retrieve his kites from nearby branches where they got tangled. He must have tried to reach a branch that seemed tantalizingly close, and lost his footing. With a few swift and giant leaps down the staircase I reached the ground where Numair's little body lay still.

There are spiritual heights viewed from which even tragedy ceases to work its tragic effect, and if we gathered all the sorrow of the world into one sorrow, who could dare to decide if a glance at it would necessarily compel or seduce us to pity...spiritual heights, one sorrow...for years now I have tried to regain my bearings with words like these...and the net result of that endeavor, still in process, makes for a story that has no end. "Numair, Numair," Ayesha cried, kneeling beside the boy, pulling his head on to her lap. Before anyone else could reach us, suddenly she raised her tear-streaked face, and flashing a belligerent look at me, she said, "We'll tell them you weren't on the roof." To this day, I don't know what sparked her to say such a thing in those first moments of terror. Did she mean only to protect me from any responsibility, or did she mean that we possibly couldn't tell anyone the truth of why we failed to watch over Numair? Within seconds the cook, then the driver, and finally her mother rushed out. They were upon us; I had no time even to tell Ayesha if I agreed with her decision. The frantic chaos of an emergency took over...and then in the coming days, the shock and the sorrow of the tragedy enveloped everyone, and by then Ayesha's account had become established. Ayesha and I never spoke about the incident again. We barely looked at each other until the burial. An enormous distance was opening up between us. She didn't give me a chance to speak to her alone. The few times I went to her place during the mourning period, we sat in the living room, amidst other relatives and visitors, practically like strangers. Then I stopped going to her house altogether, and it was Raqib who informed me of her early departure for London. I see Ayesha in my memories, and improbably often in my dreams. I see her laughing and everything she gave me – all of it appears still intact, but on another shore so incredibly far away that I can never hope to reach it again.

The Happiest Day of His Life

I didn't manage to keep up with my old classmates much, so naturally I was surprised when Amjad's letters came to me after he killed himself. I was out of the country when it happened, and heard the details, as far as they could be ascertained, from Badal, who came to deliver the letters. Badal kept up with everyone. He was just the type: energetic for someone so fat, a bit disheveled, always in a hurry, between things.

Badal liked to bring people together, to reminisce about old times. When things were good. I found these gatherings interminably boring. I didn't think the best time of my life was behind me. In fact, I was quite miserable through school and college. I had no freedom, no money, and studied hard in the hopes of having the kind of position I had today. I was having my best time now.

I had become the General Manager of Marketing and Sales for Cailler, a newly arrived multi-national. We sold chocolates and desserts; we were just starting to manufacture locally. I liked going to the headquarters in Zurich for training, or to Bombay to shoot new ads. I had finally bought my own flat in Lalmatia. My wife Rita was kind, efficient, and joyful; she kept a great house and was a superb mother. My boy, aged five and obsessed with dragons, went to the finest English-medium school.

Why would I want to sit around with a bunch of middle-aged malcontents and pretend that I was happy in the days when our only pleasure was to cut school and go on meaningless drives or watch porn if somebody's house was empty?

Still, I attended Badal's little parties—a dinner at a newly opened restaurant or a boat-trip in winter—every now and then. Badal was relentless, he had no capacity to be offended, and no number of rebuffs could stop the invitations, phone calls, personal imploration. Besides, I didn't particularly mind seeing these old friends, as long as it was at appropriate intervals. It was at one of Badal's shindigs that I last saw Amjad.

Right after I got back from a fair in Dubai, Badal came by one day to give me the news. He was not sweaty and breathless as usual, but a little morose. He had come bearing an odd little packet, which he had placed delicately on the corner of my desk, and readjusted from time to time. He had just finished telling me details of the grisly affair—bus, Airport Road—details I didn't really want to know. If someone kills himself, that may say something about them. I am not sure the manner of killing says much.

Clearly, though, Badal needed to rehearse the details, by now perfected through repetition. I assumed benevolently that repeating them brought him some solace; more unkindly one could say he asserted a kind of importance by posing as a prime custodian of this narrative. He sat across the table from me in the air-conditioned calm of my office, directly across the hall from our Bolivian M.D., fiddling with the packet that was yet to be explained.

"What I don't get," said Badal with a hint of annoyance, "is why Amjad didn't come to one of us."

"Perhaps he himself didn't realize how deeply troubled he was," I tried to suggest helpfully.

"How could he not know? He threw himself under a bus!" Badal said with rising annoyance. "Surely, this wasn't a sudden notion. Something drove him to this."

"May be he was just depressed. Sometimes there is no specific cause," I tried to explain again.

"How do you know that? You hardly kept in touch with him. I saw him a week before he died, he wasn't depressed," said Badal emphatically.

"So, what do you think it was?" I asked.

"That's the damndest thing. There's no clue. Amjad led the quietest life. What could have gone wrong?" said Badal.

"What is this?" I asked, pointing to the packet.

"It might be our only clue," said Badal, pushing the packet across the shiny glass-top table towards me. It was a little bundle—a frayed, brown envelope tied with a red and white string. Only a government office, the kind where Amjad passed his cheerless work hours, would still have such strings and envelopes. It seemed to contain some letters, not more than ten or twelve sheets from the look of it.

"Why haven't you opened it?" I asked, before noticing that my nickname was written across the top with a black marker. Even friends didn't use that name much anymore.

"He sent it to you. Monem was his best friend. Or, so we all thought. They saw each other more often than any of us did. He didn't leave this to Monem. Or, even me. It's addressed to you," said Badal, with a look that seemed to say, you be the judge of this unjust parting gesture.

I couldn't blame Badal, or Monem, or anyone else, if they felt offended that Amjad had entrusted any final missives to someone like me, who had been quite distant from him, and indeed the whole group, for years. It was not clear to me why I should be the recipient of such a dubious honor. Apparently it was found in Amjad's bag at the scene; Badal was of course the first person there. He had showed exemplary restraint and rectitude in passing on this envelope unopened to its proper addressee.

But now Badal sat staunchly in his chair, perhaps expecting me to open the envelope in his presence. I lied that I had a meeting with the M.D., and tucked the little bundle into my drawer, and locked it shut. I'd contact him, I said, if I found out any clues.

Curiosity is an odd thing. Several days passed, but I did not open the envelope from Amjad. I cannot explain what held me back. Was it a fear of finding out something undesirable about this old friend who had come to mean so little lately, but had been so close once upon a time? The knowledge of some dark revelation, within grasp and with some rights on my attention, was disturbing to live with. I slept badly, and lacked intensity in sales meetings. Nothing escaped my wife; I blamed my distraction on an imminent product launch. It seemed to suffice.

On the way to or from work, when I usually scanned the newspapers, I thought of Amjad. I know it is customary to classify most suicides into one of two categories. Either they are said to have been always so happy and successful, and consequently the life-taking is declared a mystery. Or, they are said to have been always little depressed and withdrawn, and the self-extinction is treated as an extreme but not improbable end for the person.

It was hard to place Amjad in either category. He was not an enthusiast like Badal, an executive like me, or an intellectual like Monem. He was quiet, but not brooding; he was social, but not effusive; he was charming, but not a charmer. He worked hard and did well enough, but he was neither ambitious nor a success. I felt hardly equipped to explain what he was really like. I had known him well a long time ago. In recent years, apart from Badal's occasions, I saw him only when he came to my office. I wasn't entirely sure why he came, but he had always been a rather prim and pleasant person. I have never seen anyone with so neat and precise a parting in his hair; it shone between the gelled and unmoving parts of his hair as if the scalp was made of perfect white wax. I did not mind sharing a cup of imported coffee with him.

Given the manner of his exit, I felt I didn't know him at all. But even this line of thinking seemed faulty. Perhaps I had known him as well and correctly as any person can know a friend at that age, but people change. I didn't know exactly who he had become, still I felt sure that he had not killed himself because of some tawdry, specific cause:

no betrayal, blackmail, debts, et cetera. It was something else, but I had no idea what.

One evening after everyone had cleared our floor–I was often the last one out, except the peon who closed up after me–I sat at my desk and brought out Amjad's envelope. There were, as I had suspected, only ten or twelve sheets. Judging from the variety of the papers, and the varying stages of their decay, they had been written over time at great intervals. Not a single sheet was dated, nor entirely full of text; rather they were written in the manner of aphorisms, if not poetry.

The first sheet read:

Last week on the way back from office, I decided on a whim not to take the bus. I walked instead, towards the river. I wasn't sure how far it was, or exactly where to turn. I ended up in some part of the city that I didn't quite know. The sky went dark, and streetlights came on. For the first time in ages, since I was a child, I was lost. It took a combination of buses and scooters to get back home, well past midnight. I wished I had stayed out the whole night. The few hours I was lost, sitting on the ledge of somebody's ground floor window, watching people go by, I remember that as the happiest hours I've known in a long time.

The second sheet read:

I think often of when I was happy. It is not now, I know that. I think of my childhood and I know it was not then. My father was a tyrant. If I could remember when I was last happy, perhaps I could be happy again. I can only remember fragments of days that have been happy. Sitting in class one day, watching it rain, while the teacher droned on about the Ode to something. The football field filled up with puddles. Half-naked boys who grazed cows there splashed around in the water. A weight lifted off my shoulders, why or how, I don't know. But I felt it lift, and I felt so light until the bell rang.

These scraps were so strange, so meaningless, that I skipped forward to see if there was any current or factual information anywhere. But they were all the same. Fragments of a diary, or perhaps letters to oneself, or of some kind of an intended composition. They were all the same. All of them recalled some peculiar, small moment of Amjad's life, when he had experienced a brief respite from whatever gloom hung over him. I had never suspected that within himself he harbored such a sense of oppression. I doubt if anyone did.

Not once did he mention his wife or his child. He mentioned no achievements. He didn't have many, but he did have the usual ones–graduation, first job, several promotions. There were no mention of trips or vacations–I remembered he had brought me a little carving from Madras. No special days–marriage, birthdays–and, not even calamities, or the relief of averting them, had found place in these distillations of his life as he saw it. Apparently, he had suffered all the usual vicissitudes of life indifferently. He was after something else. He had clearly not found it. But, why task me, of all people, to detect what that was?

In one of the fragments he had written, "*Sometimes I think of asking my friends about the happiest day of their lives. I don't think they will tell me.*" Is this why he came to my office from time to time? Was this what he wanted to know? It was absurd! We were modern, practical men. We did not talk of such things. We complained about all the petty irritations and indignities of life, we commiserated over the big blows with practiced fluency. But we did not go beyond the established customs of conversation.

I threw the bundle down on my desk with a feeling of exasperation. Amjad had no right to send me these letters–if that was what they were. It was rude, if not unfriendly, to leave an old acquaintance with such a paltry and bizarre set of clues to so grave an act.

I went to the washroom to splash some cold water over my face. After I came down, I let the driver go. I thought I'd drive myself. Once on the road, I didn't quite feel like going home. I drove aimlessly towards the emptier parts of the city, not daring to leave it entirely. I knew how upset Rita got if I was late for dinner without good reason. I drove around for a while with the window down, necktie removed, allowing the cool breeze of an October evening to ruffle my hair.

I managed to avoid Badal for a couple of weeks. I didn't know what to tell him. I had read the letters again since I first opened them. As I re-read them, certain aspects of my friendship with Amjad returned to mind. Amjad, Monem, and I were more speculative than the others. We read some of the books that people read at that age, and asked the questions that people ask after reading those books. What made for a good or meaningful life? Could a happy life be meaningful as well? What if the two diverged?

Like most well-adjusted adults, I had left those questions behind, decisively, a long time ago. Amjad was clearly more vulnerable than we were.

"You are so hard to get a hold of," Badal said, wiping his brow with a purple sleeve, when he finally managed to trap me in my office again.

We talked desultorily about our respective works. He was planning to bring a hot Uzbek dance troupe to town. It would be a smash hit, he was convinced. Something special with which to kick off the winter season.

When I didn't bring up Amjad's letters for half an hour, Badal could contain himself no more. "So, what he did have to say for himself, that stupid, selfish bastard?"

I couldn't blame Badal for his impatience. It was he who had raised the money to prevent Amjad's widow from being evicted.

"Nothing, really. It was just some fragments from his diary," I said. "No clues."

"Can I see it?"

"I'm afraid not. He had instructed me to burn it after I read it," I lied.

Badal looked a little disappointed. "Oh well, nothing he had to say would do anybody any good now, would it?"

"Quite so," I said.

Badal got up to leave, and I walked him to the door. But, just before he stepped out, I grabbed his arm and asked, "Listen, tell me something. Are you happy?"

"I'm too busy to be happy or unhappy, man," Badal said with his booming laugh. "Why what's the matter with you? Are you okay?"

"Oh, of course, I am just fine," I said with a smile, relaxing my grip.

"Don't worry, I'm not going over the edge. And don't you do something like that either. One a season is enough, don't you think?"

"Yes, quite enough," I said, laughing with Badal, as he stormed off to his next social prey.

That night I came home late. I had gone off on a drive again. It had become a new habit of mine. I don't know why I didn't tell Rita that this was what I did. It was so harmless. When I entered the flat, I could tell that everyone was asleep. My dinner was covered on the table with a note that said, "Help yourself." I knew I was in trouble. I walked in my socks to our room and found it empty. I spied Rita with our boy, in his room, both fast asleep. I stared at them from the door, ghostly figures in the blue nightlight. As I watched their small bodies rise softly with each breath, I knew I loved them. At the same time, for all my love, I also knew that in this moment, to me, they were both strangers.

Good Night, Mr. Kissinger

The first time I met Henry Kissinger, I was shocked at how frail he appeared. Of course, "met" is a strong word when you are a waiter. But waiters in restaurants of a certain elevation, like butlers or barbers of another era, enjoy a strange though controlled intimacy with the men they serve.

At a place like The Solstice, it is almost expected for a good waiter to get past the menu with repeat visitors. Once in the middle of a conversation with a silver-haired lawyer, Kissinger was groping for the name of the capital of Tajikistan. It was a delicate call; I took a chance: Dushanbe.

"What is your name?" Mr. Kissinger asked me with slight bemusement.

"James, sir. James D' Costa."

"Where are you from?"

"Bangladesh, sir."

"A James from Bangladesh? An unlikely name for a Bangladeshi, isn't it?"

"It's an unlikely country, sir," I replied as I swept away the crumbs from the thick white tablecloth.

Encounters with the famous and the mighty was one of the great perks of my otherwise often tiring job: politicians, movie stars, authors, sports heroes, socialites. Just the week before meeting Kissinger, I had witnessed the daughter of a real-estate tycoon storm out in tears over a breakup. A month before that I had to find a spare pair of trousers for a druggy star who had soiled himself in the men's room. I was moved by the graciousness of Gregory Peck and charmed by the sweetness of the Queen of Jordan. Once I pulled Harvey Weinstein away—I am an exceptionally big man for a Bangladeshi—when he struck a young director who had crossed him. Yet, somehow the little repartee with Kissinger felt like the highlight.

When I brought the check to Kissinger, he asked me, "So how is your unlikely country doing these days?"

"Quite well, sir," I replied, trying to stay neutral.

"It can't be doing that well if you are here, can it? How long have you been in America?"

"Just two years, sir."

"I hope your country isn't still a basket-case for the sake of those who are stuck there," said Mr. Kissinger, as he wrote in a fat sum for the tip.

Clearly, I had not been forgiven for Dushanbe. But the insult was excessive. The dessert knife, still on the table, flashed before my eyes. Kissinger's neck was soft and crumply enough that I could have pierced it with a blunt instrument. I have always been given to sudden and extreme bursts of rage, though I try not to act on them. The last time I did, I had to leave the country. I removed myself from the scene with a brusque "Thank you," leaving the farewell ritual to a smooth-faced actor amenable to my bullying.

As far as the American immigration service is concerned, I am a political refugee. The real circumstances of my departure are of course more complicated. I used to be an English teacher at a private college in Dhaka. One would not expect a character like me to become a teacher. I harked back to British times when tough guys became teachers, and ran gymnasiums to train young anti-colonial radicals. I doubled up as the games teacher for my college. Not the pot-bellied, whistle-blowing kind. I taught the boys how to dodge and tackle, taking hard falls with them in the rain-sodden field on summer afternoons.

I felt free to egress into unnecessary territories. Anytime the faculty had a new need–not something as grubby as a salary-increase–but a new line of acquisitions for the library or an expansion of the common room, I would lead the negotiations. I chided the peons when they slacked off on keeping the bathrooms and corridors clean. I bullied the bullies among the students. I could have asserted myself in a bigger arena, but felt content with the little theater of my college. I enjoyed scolding socially well-placed but negligent parents.

In addition to temperament, I was helped in my subtle transgressions by sheer physical size. I was big not just for a Bengali, but for almost any nationality. I could crack open a hard coconut shell with the back of my fist. I used this trick to awe the newcomers and to intimidate any challengers. I should have known that my predilections destined me for trouble. A student, whom I had failed, begged first for re-grading, then re-examination. Then he grew bolder, offering veiled threats. Violence has become so common in Dhaka that everyone knows a two-bit goon and feels free to lean on that assumed advantage. I slapped the boy hard and told him to focus on his studies. A few days later, I spotted a clownish trio, wearing gold-chains and sunglasses, dawdling outside the college gate. They leaned against their 100cc Japanese bike as if it were a Harley.

I found their posture comic and paid no heed to their hard stares. But a few weeks later when I was returning home, they fell upon me without any warning or preamble, just as I turned the corner onto the dark alley leading to my house. I took a cut to my chin, but managed to wrestle away a bicycle chain from one of their hands. The student was the slowest to escape. I chased him down and with one metallic swish from behind caught him across the face. I should have stopped right there; but I could not forgive a student who would dare raise a hand against a teacher.

The fact that I had acted in self-defense, even if excessively, was completely overlooked in the ensuing uproar. A few students began a boycott of my classes, and a few parents pressed for an investigation. My defense grew weaker as the boy, now the victim, languished in a hospital. Within a week, no students attended my classes. The authorities asked me to take leave pending an investigation. Old stories about my prowess and vigilance circulated with sinister exaggerations. The boy's parents pressed criminal charges. I did not have the appetite for the legal fight, nor for the humiliations needed to resolve the issue out of court. I managed to secure an American visa, and upon landing filed for asylum. It helped that I was a Christian with a record of secular activism from a country growing ever more radical.

When I say I am given to sudden rage, it is not entirely accurate. I have always lived in a state of seething rage, but its focus has shifted over the years. Targets receded while new obsessions bloomed. As a child, if the cooking was not to my liking, I would hurl the bowl of curry at the wall and watch the yellow sauce dribble down our much-stained wall. In a developed country they might have submitted me to some form of treatment or counseling. Back home I received vigorous thrashings from my father, but I lost him too early in life to know if his admonishments might have made a difference.

During the war of liberation I was only nine. My father, pastor of a small church on the outskirts of Dhaka, was shot dead by the Pakistanis. The soldiers invaded our house early one morning. Somehow the army skipped our town in the first days of war, when Dhaka was massacred. But a couple of months later, they entered our town blaring the message that anyone who lived peacefully and cooperated would be unharmed. The next morning they came for my father, the first operation in our town.

I remember that ten or twelve soldiers had entered our little compound. I imagine more surrounded the house and guarded the arched gateway of our very old house. My father came out to the verandah, already bent in submission, appeasement dripping from his voice. That's what I remember most vividly. The image of my father on his knees, shirt open, pleading for his family. My mother and I watched from behind a door. My mother held my one-year old brother to her breast. The child, sensing disorder, began to bawl. Luckily, the soldiers were not interested in us. They had come specifically for my father, who they believed was aiding insurgents. Having ensured that there were none hiding in our house, they left us alone.

One soldier stood by the gate, under the old Arjun tree, with a leer on his broad square face. In a moment like that your comprehension can transcend your age and become universal. I knew even at that age, and in that moment, that the soldier was not smiling with malice, but out of idiocy. He fired suddenly at a goat that leapt out of the vegetable patch at one end of our compound. The major leading the operation blasted a series of expletives at the idiot soldier and ordered him out. Then he turned and barked another order, and my father was shot ten or twenty times, I can't remember, even after his body had gone still on the ground.

Many details of that morning are no longer vivid in my mind. I don't remember if it was a cloudy morning, or which neighbor was the first to rush over once the soldiers left. What I remember vividly is the shaking, kneeling figure of my father, and the smiling face of the idiot soldier. Where is he now? I wondered as I grew older. What if I went to Karachi or Lahore some day, and found him behind the counter of a store?

My unstable moods, in the absence of my father, grew more volatile for a period. Especially in my teenage years, I got into scrapes constantly. I spent almost as much time in suspension as in class. I daydreamed, not of girls, or football, or cars, or anything teenagers commonly fantasize about, but of revenge. I drafted elaborate plans to execute the killers of 1971. It would not be necessary to kill all the culprits; I required only symbolic justice.

Yet, justice was the only thing that my country failed to deliver. I became involved in secularist politics after democracy was restored in the early '90s. I organized awareness-raising events in small towns. But, to my dismay, once in power, even the liberals succumbed to compromise. Eventually the killers and collaborators became ministers. I gave up on wider political work, and became increasingly concerned with upholding vestiges of order and dignity in the immediate and small arena of my college, until, of course, things went too far.

The move to America seemed to calm my spirits. Or, my shaky legal status in an alien land had a restraining effect on my temper. We had sold the old family property to raise the money for my passage. I blew much of that fund on a rental deposit for a one-bedroom in Sunnyside, Queens. My brother, who didn't mind selling the house for my safety, was irritated when he heard of this move. The few contacts from home I met, and later avoided, advised me against it. But having spent the first few weeks with six young Bengali taxi-drivers in a two-bedroom, I was sure I wanted my own space. I had never lived alone before in thirty-seven years. I couldn't believe how good it felt.

I liked being alone when I woke up, and when I went to sleep. I could see living alone for the rest of my life. I had loved girls, and I had been loved back. But the one girl I might have married, I lost for reasons I still don't understand. I felt no strong need for companionship at this time. I worked one long shift from noon to ten at night. I liked having much of the mornings to myself. To go sit at the diner by the station, with a paper, made for a morning hour more delicious than any I had known before. I liked the smell of coffee, and I liked how in this country they topped it up endlessly.

While my work was not easy, I had it easier than many of my countrymen. I could not pass by any Bangladeshi fruit-seller on winter mornings without a shiver of pity for them, and thankfulness for my luck. My move up the restaurant ladder to The Solstice was rapid, thanks mainly to my English and general quickness. I enjoyed learning about the great wines of the world–the difference between a Petrus Pomerol 1998 and an ordinary $100 Merlot– appealed to some arcane aspect of my temperament. I loved the elaborateness of our accoutrements, the hierarchy, the rituals, and the art of effacing it all into a seamless, effortless performance. Here, finally, was a civilized order.

I was never desperate, like millions of my countrymen, to leave Bangladesh. I had never given serious thought to emigration, never explored any such options. Yet trading the chaos and violence of Dhaka for the relative calm and order of New York felt like a boon. My new city, like my place of work, offered me a world of rules. In return, I needed to keep my overdeveloped sense of dignity under check. Surprisingly, this task came as a huge relief. No longer did I have to measure every smile, look, or gesture, nor constantly defend myself against the slightest omissions of respect.

I felt no great longing to go back to Dhaka, even for a visit. Of course, I missed aspects of Dhaka. I missed the Kal Boishakhi rains that heralded summer with a sudden and terrible lash of winds and hail. I missed dal puris with hot tea at the stall by my college on foggy winter mornings. But on the whole, I was happier in my new life. The owner of a Bangladeshi restaurant in Astoria approached me at regular intervals to teach at a public school loaded with Bangladeshis. The man was a busybody who took an interest in community affairs. "The boys and girls need a Bangladeshi teacher, a role model. Someone strong and good in English." Sometimes he came to see me with sidekicks to add weight to his appeal.

"Surely you know why I left home?" I said to dissuade the man.

"People there always overreact and exaggerate," said the man gallantly. "I pay no heed to rumors."

Clearly, they were desperate for a good teacher. But I was not moved by their need or flattery. To accept their offer would mean getting drawn into the community, and the politics and issues from home. I did not wish to have any old feelings stirred up. But I should have known that it is not easy to leave worlds behind. Just when I thought I had fully bulwarked myself against my past, it ambushed me from a completely unexpected direction, in the unlikely figure of Henry Kissinger.

Like all educated Bangladeshis, I held Kissinger culpable to some degree for the genocide that occurred in my country in 1971. I knew that he did not order it, but I also knew that he did nothing to discourage his Pakistani clients, though he wielded enormous influence on them. These were issues I had gladly left behind. Yet, suddenly now the issue was palpably before me, demanding to be fed and humored.

I hoped the second time Kissinger saw me, since it was already several weeks from our first meeting, that he would not remember me. Instead, as soon as I brought him the menu, he greeted me affably, "James, right? From Bangladesh?"

"You are very kind to remember, sir," I said trying to put on my best faux-English politeness. It worked well with the older crowd.

"James is a bit of a student of world politics, even geography, if I remember correctly," said Kissinger to a budding blonde newswoman who was his dinner companion that night.

"Again, you are too kind, sir. May I bring you some water? Or, call the sommelier?"

"Sure, sure, there will be time enough for all that. Tell me first what you think of this terrible attack," said the old man easing into a winged leather chair. The old fox was not to be diverted easily. Once during the meal, and then again when I brought him the check, he tried to trap me into political talk. I would not have expected Kissinger to be the kind of big man who engages underlings, let alone service staff, in chats of any kind. But clearly I piqued some perverse interest in him.

I persuaded the head waiter to assign me to the front part of the restaurant, adjoining the bar-lounge area. They preferred to have the good-looking actors work that area. People like me, people with personality, we were told, were needed in the main dining room, where the more demanding older customers were usually seated. Luckily the head waiter, a bushy-browed, gay Englishman of great Old World charm, had taken a liking to me, and I managed to get my area changed.

The next time Kissinger walked in, I could watch him with relief from a distance. I was talking a young couple into ordering our hideously over-priced special of the night–a Kobe Wagyu beef with cockle clams Agar Agar in a seaweed soy sauce. It was the latest invention of our famous Spanish Chef, a diva of insufferable proportions. In the middle of my sale, suddenly I felt a tap on my shoulder. It was the head waiter with a twinkle in his old eyes.

"Kissinger asked for you," he murmured in my ear, and turning to the young couple in his cheeriest tone, "May I continue taking your orders, please?"

This was more interest than I expected or required from Kissinger. No doubt the man had a streak of sadism in him. He would not stop pestering me with probing questions about the state of my country. One day he asked me if I thought it was a matter of time before a Bangladeshi would be caught in a terror attempt.

"Why just attempt, sir, why not an actual attack?" I blurted out, on the verge of losing control.

"I can't imagine they would have the competence, can you?" said Kissinger with a smile.

I could feel the vein in my scalp throb. I placed the wine bottle back in its silver bucket before I was tempted to swing it down on Kissinger's face. After that second encounter, I could not stop thinking about harming Kissinger. Not since my teenage years, had anyone or anything sparked such sustained fantasies of violence in me. A steak knife would of course be the obvious choice of weapon in this context. I was not sure I would be entirely beyond committing such a bizarre attack.

My entire past, I realized looking back from the calm perch of my new life, was strewn with acts of petty violence. I used physical force to impose my will, whenever my personality or reasoning was not enough. It came easily with people against whom a certain degree of violence was permissible in my culture–students, servants, urchins, neighborhood toughs. But I pushed the boundaries of even other relationships. Once I took a rude parent by the arm to walk him out of my room. I banged on the table of my startled principal to make points. Another time I shook a policeman almost senseless for trying to shakedown my scooter-driver. All those actions–more than I could actually list–pointed inevitably towards the excess of my last action.

So many people in the world–from Chile to Cambodia–had a case at least as justified as mine against Kissinger, yet was I the first to have access both to his enemy and to dangerous weapons at the same time and place? How many times had he been exposed to the possibility of a stray, lunatic assault?

Kissinger came to The Solstice at least once a month; usually for dinner, and never failed to engage me in what he must have considered friendly banter.

If I really wanted to hurt him, all I would have to do is wait for his next visit. I would watch him from the bridge to the serving station, eyes glazed and lower lip hanging, signs of a glutton, or just age, slowly passing morsels of rich food from his plate to his mouth on the tips of a silver fork. I could snatch that fork away and stab him in the eye faster than any security man could bat an eyelid. Besides, they were easily distracted with a plate of appetizers. Realizing that I had him in my hands seemed to have a calming effect on me. No matter what impertinent comments he made, I thought to myself, Old man, you have no idea how close you are to danger!

I wondered if he was rude to people from every country whose independence he had opposed. Or, did he detect some streak of defiance beneath the veneer of my professional politeness, which prompted him to make rude remarks about my country? I expected the animal instinct to be strong in a man like him. Instead of outright injury, I toyed with the idea of insults. Splashed wine, stinging slap.

The more I thought about it, I also realized that no injury I could cause him would get either Kissinger himself or the world to see him as I wished. Still, part of me wanted to be provoked to the point of explosion, no matter what the outcome. Could you get deported for mouthing off to a former Secretary of State? Could such rashness be construed as a threat to national security?

Of course, even the slightest of actions entertained in my fantasies would cost me my job, if not land me in jail. For all my pride, I found that that was deterrent enough. I didn't understand why life's restraints worked so well on people like me, but not on the likes of Kissinger. Why can some people literally get away with murder, becoming ministers or dining on Pemaquid Oysters, while we can only stew in impotent rage?

I chose as a sign of protest the habit of leaving it to other waiters to see Kissinger off. I refused to pull his chair or fetch his coat. Dodging these tasks became an art, made easy by the fact that four other waiters were perfectly happy to step in for a big man. The head waiter himself loved attending to his biggest clients so much that he did not seem to notice that I was absconding from my proper role.

I started working fewer nights, having finally relented to offer private lessons to some Bangladeshi students. Some of them struggled to pass high school, while others strove to earn good scholarships. These tuitions paid very little, but I found that they formed a good balance with my restaurant job. Instead of cursing Kissinger all the way back from work on the 7 train, I jotted down little points for the next day's lessons. I was sure I could get many more of my students qualified for college than they seemed to think possible.

I had saved up enough money to buy a place of my own, though I chose to send it back to my brother. I told them to buy an apartment in Dhaka. I started taking a Bangla paper now and then to my diner in the mornings; football scores of teams I once rooted for brought a strange glow of warmth to my heart. The novelty of meeting a figure like Kissinger began to fade. He stopped seeming like history embodied. I began to realize the impossibility of finding satisfaction in the event of a great wrong. I asked my students, during a lesson on the Liberation War, "Can you forgive those who don't even know that they need to be forgiven?" I drew blank stares and diverted the discussion to other topics.

I thought of writing a letter to the student whom I had hurt. Even though I was sure he could never forgive me.

Kissinger's provocations did not abate. I see you have once again topped the list for corruption. What is it with your people? Don't you really think it might do better as a province of India? The man's capacity for offense was endless. But his comments could not touch me anymore. Indeed, when he came to The Solstice soon after the Bangladeshi Independence Day, I reminded him of the fact, knowing full well he might use it as an opening. "Not much to show for thirty some years, except billions in aid and debt."

"So it would seem from afar, Mr. Kissinger. But not up close," I contradicted, taking a chance. At any rate, the man's predictability amused me.

That night I finally saw him off. I fetched his coat and opened the door, towering over his short, stooped figure, moving slowly under heavy layers.

"Thank you, James," said Kissinger, as he stepped into the cold March night for the warm cabin of a waiting limousine.

"Good night, Mr. Kissinger," said I, drawing the door of the Solstice behind him to a close.

The Year of Return

Like so many people my age, and from a country like mine, I too lived abroad as a young man. My life abroad was not too atypical: a first degree from Toronto, a stint of work in Vancouver, a second degree from Chicago and a longer stint of work in San Francisco. My career was marked by a few small deviations from the familiar script. I traveled on work to the Caribbean, where I met a half-Indian, half-French girl, whom I made the mistake of marrying. I tried hang gliding, because not many South Asians do. For a while I tried to get a wine cellar going, but grew tired of the people one meets in that line of diversion.

The reasons for my return were not unheard-of either: My father had passed away, and my mother–though still diligent about her ladies' lunches and Mah-jongg–was starting to complain. Additionally, my wife left me for a Cuban musician in Los Angeles, taking our four- year-old daughter and a big chunk of my assets with her. I got laid off twice, and found out it took ever longer to get placed. The kind of work I did–financial analysis–people did for a lot cheaper in the part of world I had come from.

I didn't visit much while I was away. I thought I was coming back to the city of my childhood, only bigger, busier, more congested and polluted. Through all my sojourns, I was comforted by the knowledge that there was a place I could always go back to. Even if I did not think

of Dhaka as a whole as home, certainly Dhanmondi existed in my mind
as my very own place. I had no idea what I was getting back to.

Six months after I had come home, one day a letter arrived in my
name. The envelope was a bit dirty. The letter was anonymous. The
message simple: "Give us 5 million takas within three days or we will
blow your brains out." I had never received an extortion letter before, let
alone a death threat. I felt no fear or urgency reading this message; it felt
quite remote. It didn't seem like it could have anything to do with me.

I did not tell my mother about this letter. Nor did I think about it
much for the next two days. On the third day, I got a phone call.

"Is this Andalib Khan?"

"Yes, speaking."

"Have you done anything to organize the money?"

"Who is this?"

"You know very well who this is. It's the Angel of Death, you pussy-
faced little shit. Have the money ready tomorrow."

"Where am I supposed to get so much money suddenly? I think
you've got the wrong person."

"I'll give you till the end of the week," said the person before
hanging up.

There was nothing here at first: a four hundred-year-old mosque
and paddy fields. Then my grandfather arrived after the Partition in
his Jeep, with a double-barrel shotgun. The area was so pristine back
then, you had to arrange your own protection. One by one came the
others. The neighborhood filled up with lovely one- or two-story houses with wide verandahs, coconut trees, and Krishnachuras lining the
boundaries.

Today most of the old houses are gone. Now and then, one spots
a relic, abandoned by the original settlers of Dhanmondi, wedged between the towering new apartment blocks with their shiny steel and
glass facades and ridiculous names–Millennium Housing, Phoenix

Towers, Greenview Apartments. What green view? All the beautiful trees have been cut.

Our house is one of the relics. I stand on my verandah every morning with a cup of steaming tea, in my shirt and tie, before heading out to the bank where I am a vice-president. I watch the people go by and wonder where they have come from. Not one of them looks like they belong here.

The city is full of neighborhoods and people that didn't exist when I was growing up. I hear strange new names–Paikpara, Bhasantek, Kuril, Merul–and have no idea where these places are. I imagine vast, sprawling slums. The condemned spill into neighborhoods like mine. They envy what we have and become filled with a desire to seize it or destroy it. I can't blame them.

In the one year that I have been back, I have counted at least a half dozen violent incidents within close proximity. Soon after I arrived, a client was shot by hijackers trying to snatch a bag of cash right outside our bank. A few months later, robbers threw a bomb at a chasing mob, disemboweling one vigilante. One night a man was shot dead by the lake, right in front of my house, while we were at dinner. I didn't know a gunshot could sound so small.

In the face of the rising crimes and anarchy, I was always calm, until the day I received that letter. I worried that the thugs might call when my mother was home alone. I did what people do in a situation like this. I called a friend.

Shamim was one of the few friends from my schooldays with whom I still had a connection. He too had gone abroad, to become a barrister from London, but he had returned long before I did. He dabbled on the fringes of party politics. He knew his way around the city. At first, Shamim said that prank calls like this were quite common. Then he paused and asked me, "Aren't you planning to sell the old house? Who else knows that you are selling the house?"

"Anyone who knows me could know; it's not a secret."

"It should have been. It was a mistake. See, if you had been back at least a year now, you would have known better. You would not have made such an elementary mistake. Anyway, what's done is done. You haven't sold it already, have you?"

"No, but I might be close to selling."

"Whoever called knows what's happening. You better talk to someone who can deal with such things."

This was how I got back in touch with Badshah.

Badshah was also a friend from our schooldays. But he came from a different background than people like Shamim or myself. Badshah lived in Mohammadpur, in a dirty yellow building. His father was a schoolteacher. When we left to study abroad, Badshah enrolled in a local Degree College.

The first time I met Badshah again, after all these years, I was truly surprised at how easy it was to talk with him. It is easier to overcome disparate backgrounds when you are a child, and again as you get older. Youth is very discriminating; superficialities take over. But now, we talked again just like old friends.

Badshah's life had not gone the way I had imagined it might. He had not entered government service or tried to scrape through a medical college in a provincial town. He had become an enterprising success—a few lines of buses, road works, a cable service. All of these in partnership, mostly with mid-ranking politicians. He exuded the confidence of a successful man. He had married a TV starlet and confined her to the house with serial pregnancies. The city was full of men like him these days.

"So, Shamim tells me you're in trouble," said Badshah, flicking some ash into a tea cup in my non-smoking office. We were past the catching up.

"I can't even tell if it's just a hoax," I said, feeling suddenly shy; not knowing what kind of help to ask for.

"I've already investigated the matter a little. It's not a hoax. I have leads. Don't worry, I'll sort it out for you," he said matter-of-factly.

When we were in school, we were the same height and both on the thin side. I was quite a bit taller than Badshah now; having grown a few late inches in college. But Badshah had a kind of gravity that was elusive yet palpable. Neither fat nor thin, he was simply full. He filled the clothes he wore, the chair he occupied, and any room he walked into. He had narrow, unforgiving eyes that could sparkle with sudden affability. He had the thick wrists of someone who could manhandle his opponents.

Badshah took me into a side of Dhaka that was not known to me. We met at a hotel I'd never heard of, in a part of town I never visited, but they served whiskey and vodka–all genuine imports, though limited in range. The people who came to his table talked of everything–people, places, guns, drugs–in nicknames. They laughed at the grotesque inaccuracy of the stories in the papers. They knew the story behind the stories.

While Badshah's world fascinated me, I could stand to be around his cronies only so much. But Badshah had not lost his sense of subtlety, and before I had to say anything, he moved our rendezvous to the Emerald Lodge, a low-key rest house in Gulshan, where we were served in private rooms, by girls of surprising sophistication. I was never a drinking or whoring man; but somehow in Badshah's company I could not refuse these diversions.

When Shamim heard of my escapades with Badshah, he said grimly, "Don't get too close to him. He's not like us you know."

"I know he isn't like us. That's why he could solve my problem so easily," I said with a laugh.

"Don't say I didn't warn you," said Shamim.

Badshah did not strike me as dangerous, not for me. He was just an old friend who had turned out to be more interesting and useful than anyone might have predicted. It was always he who called me. He came always to my office, not to my house. In its second life, our friendship had settled into that plateau. Badshah had his hands on the gears and pullies that run a big city below the surface. There was a thrill in catching glimpses of it. Besides, I had not been able to re-establish any of the old friendships. I had been away too long. Even Shamim I saw only once every few months.

Six months had gone by since Badshah solved my problem. I had seen little of him for weeks. I had taken a trip to Los Angeles to see my daughter, who was growing up with aching rapidity. I quarreled with my ex-wife about reducing my obligations. I thought of bringing Badshah over to solve this problem, and chuckled at my own joke as I drove away from Crenshaw—it was inevitable that my ex-wife would live there. When I mentioned the riots or crime, she lectured me about the vibrant culture of that place, all the music and the clubs, and reminded me of the risks of living in Dhaka.

When I came back, Badshah called me out to the Emerald Lodge. The room was familiar, but the décor more stark. No drinks on the table, no mood lighting, no smiling girl in sight. The curtain, looking cheaper in the glare of neon overheads, moved imperceptibly from the blowing air-conditioner. Badshah himself looked preoccupied.

"Is everything all right, Badshah?" I asked, sensing that it was not.

"No, I have some troubles," he said grimly.

"But you are the great troubleshooter," I said in a feeble attempt to make things light.

"I need your help, Andalib," said Badshah, looking at me with no shred of humor in his eyes.

I was stunned. "My help? What could I possibly do for you?"

"I need money," said Badshah briskly, as if he had no time to waste.

"How much?"

"One crore," he said unblinkingly. "Give it to me as a loan," he said, after a pause, leaning back into his sofa, a ghastly green affair with large wildflower prints. Why had I never noticed before how ugly this room was?

I felt a sudden churn in my stomach, and then my throat went completely dry. I looked around for a drink of water. Badshah must have seen the color drain from my face. He walked over to the writing table to pour a glass of water for me from the decanter. Handing it to me he said, "You must have at least a crore left from the sale of the house. Surely, you're not going to ignore me in my time of need?"

"I told you don't get too close to him," said Shamim.

"You are the one who introduced me to him again," I said churlishly.

"Yes, but I didn't tell you to go whoring with him!"

I did what people do in these situations. I began to avoid Badshah. I asked for time. I tried to explain with only a shred of truth that my wife had drained me of most of the proceedings from the sale in child support and alimony. I scheduled work trips which I could have assigned to subordinates. I took my mother to Bangkok for a checkup and stayed longer than we had to. Then Badshah got hold of me one day and said, in a tone I had never heard before, "I am beginning to feel insulted. Please don't insult me. Meet me at the Lodge tonight and don't come empty-handed."

I thought of telling Shamim where and when I'd be meeting Badshah, in case I didn't come back. Then I laughed at my own sense of drama. This time Badshah was in a much better mood than when we had last met. I felt greatly relieved not only to see drinks on the table, but especially to see one of the nubile hostesses flit in and out with chips and an ice bucket with only tongs, no picks. I reassured myself with sightings of other people in the lobby, a cleaner in the corridor.

"Have you been avoiding me, Andalib?" Badshah asked with a smile that hovered in some enigmatic space between affability and threat.

My sense of ease evaporated just as quickly; I repeated the ineffectual excuses with which I had tried to fend him off all these months.

"I know you have the money," Badshah said with discomforting certainty. "I can't understand why you won't give it to me. Perhaps you don't believe me when I say it'll be a loan. I'll even return it with interest."

"It's a lot of money," I said dully.

"Of course it's a lot of money. I wouldn't have to ask you if I didn't need so much. You think I like asking a friend?"

"Are we really friends?" I asked with sudden courage.

"I thought we were real friends when you guys took off for America, England, Canada, and never wrote me a letter. Never sent me even a five-pence postcard. Until then I used to think we were friends. I couldn't get a five-minute appointment with Shamim when I was starting out. But, he found me all right when he needed me. So did you. You ask me are we real friends?" There was no heat in Badshah's voice, nor even malice. With a wave he sent away the girl who came in to fill up our glasses.

I was sitting up on the edge of my sofa. I could see him clearly for the first time. He was no killer. He was a small-timer. He was once a goon, now a con. He had some business, a family, and debts. I could see now who might have sent me that letter. I had brought five lacs with me, thinking it'd be enough to buy some more time. Now I thought fifty thousand would get rid of him for good. But I didn't want to give him even five. I wanted to give him a piece of my mind.

When I finished, Badshah just smiled. "You think I am trying to use you? You think I am a criminal? Look around you. Look at this city, this society. Even the good people, your family, everyone wants to use you. They'll never ask what you want, nor listen if you tell them. We chew each other up, suck out the marrow, then throw the bone out for someone else to lick. Why blame me alone?"

I hadn't expected such a personal outburst from him. Badshah's forehead was beaded with sweat. By the moment he was growing smaller and more human. He was emerging from the shadow of menace and sordidness that had surrounded him all these months. Or, that I had cast on him. I felt I could walk away and there was not a thing that Badshah could do to me. It was all bluff. Perhaps he'd hire an urchin to throw a brick at my car one day, nothing more.

Then two more men came into the room. They lacked Badshah's humanity. You could see in their eyes that some part of their brain was missing. They could not comprehend pain in others any more than they could comprehend any risk to themselves. This was why they made good killers. I knew they wouldn't kill me. They dragged me out of the sofa and threw me onto the floor.

I wish I could say that the anticipation was the worst part of it. But the anticipation lasted the whole time, every kick, every blow; the pauses between them were filled with suspense. Where would it land next? Instinctively, I tried to protect my face. Mercifully they didn't pry my arms open; they kicked me around lazily on whatever parts were exposed. I don't remember when Badshah walked out of the room. Nor who pulled the money out of my waistband, nor when.

I don't know why I never went to the police. I never even told Shamim what happened. I told my mother I had had a small car crash; she would not notice the car. Luckily nothing was broken; the recovery was quick. I don't know if Badshah had planned to beat me up all along. I don't know why Badshah didn't try to get more money out of me. Perhaps it's because Dhaka is such a big city now; all relationships are so transient. We make our transactions and move on.

My mother and I have moved to an apartment block–New Horizon Towers–while the builders develop our plot. I go to my bank; I have become Senior Vice-President. I talk to my daughter; her French is well past mine by now. My mother keeps up with her Mah-jongg. I keep track of the crime news in my area. I check the rearview before stepping out every time. Shamim was right; it takes at least a full year to get fully reoriented. Now, I feel at home again.

Ramkamal's Gift

Ramkamal, who claimed to be the author of the greatest novel never written, disappeared nine months ago. We couldn't be entirely sure of his disappearance, but nine months seemed a bit long even for him to manage hiding without a trace. There was no credible sighting or contact with anyone, not even in our extended circle. Yet we refused to give up hope, perhaps as much out of our love, indeed reverence, for Ramkamal, as out of a desperate longing to witness the unfolding of that great, mystical text, which we all believed him entirely capable of writing.

Bahar went looking for Ramkamal in his ancestral village and discovered no one by his name had ever lived there. Joydeep checked out the dope dens of the Bauls in Kushtia and found that the Bauls did not recognize his identity. Despite the growing unreliability of Ramkamal's stories, others roamed the city probing all possible shelters and sources: rich patrons who might be hosting Ramkamal's occultation; the Special Branch—where I had a friend—and crime reporters; massage parlors in Uttara and all-night restaurants in Sadar Ghat; the tight-lipped circle of small-time arms dealers and other illicit traders with whom Ramkamal consorted in his last days.

No one could bring back any useful clue. If you find out where he is, tell me – the jerk owes me money! That was the universal refrain of the interviews. More surprising allegations sprang forth from many corners of the city. In Kalabagan, a customs official pointed to his scalp and claimed that Ramkamal had taken his hair, promising an undelivered cure to an obscure skin disease. In Mirpur, a local hood said Ramkamal stole his gun license and he'd shoot the fucker in his eyes when he found him. In Azimpur, the searcher was greeted by a prematurely retired actress holding a baby whose eyes, disturbingly, were grayish like Ramkamal's.

I was less surprised by these findings than most of Ramkamal's protégés, partly because I was, in certain senses, not one of them. I was more of a friend and almost the same age as Ramkamal. We met a few years ago—though it feels like eons—at the burial of a famous poet. Ramkamal stood, a little apart from the crowd, his long, jut-jawed face looking impassively grave. He leaned his sinewy body, tightly clad in a white T-shirt, against a shimul tree, blowing little puffs of smoke from a filterless cigarette. The red Keds, a signature item, as I'd find out in time, echoed the red blaze of the shimuls. Despite an air of self-composed authority, I detected a certain tension about him that intrigued me. So, I approached him and asked, "Were you close to the deceased?"

"No, not at all," said Ramkamal. "He was a really bad writer. I came to be sure that they buried him."

From that first encounter I knew that Ramkamal was a fellow from whom one could always expect a bit of the unexpected. Once they started chucking dollops of earth onto the grave, Ramkamal and I walked away. We went to a restaurant in Kataban that Ramkamal knew and ordered two glasses of cold lemon juice. It wasn't much of a place: a clutter of scratched-up pink Formica tables in a dark little room and an AC that produced more noise than cool air.

Ramkamal could give a convincing impression of talking about himself, even when he revealed little, factually, about his life. He talked about literature, that is, what was wrong with it and those who produced it. All the genres are now out-dated, and the ones suitable for this age are yet to emerge, he said. He could make pronouncements like that with a straight face, and as if it mattered. He refused to discuss any literature only within its own tradition. There was no scope for any writer in the modern period–meaning since the invention of steamboats–to pretend that they did not know the frontiers that had been already breached in world literature. This was why he refused to forgive Tagore's novels. He dismissed much of what passed as literature in Bengali, barring bright exceptions like the poets of the '30s, or individual texts of a Waliullah or a Jahir. He disdained the provincial self-regard, the pieties, and the sentimentalities. It's all so false and timid, pretending to be deep or holy, when it is really nothing but middle class pettiness and delusion, he said.

I hardly noticed when our lemon juice had been replaced with cold, cheap, odious vodka. Apparently, it was the only place in Kataban that kept a secret stash, and served only to a few chosen customers like Ramkamal.

Ramkamal's ideas were not new to me, but the sense of urgency was refreshing. I'd been around literary types practically all my life. Literature was my truest love. I started collecting books when I was ten. I studied English in university, under the misguided notion that the professors would share my passion. They turned out to be glorified clerks, who cared only about their salaries and about quoting other professors. I puttered around in publishing and editorial roles in my twenties, until I set up my own bookstore. I knew I couldn't write, but I could not stop wanting to keep transacting with the written world. I didn't particularly enjoy the people who were drawn to this world. They tended to be broken, touchy, and insufferable. More pitiful, than despicable, but annoying nonetheless. Ramkamal seemed free from such afflictions. He was a being possessed with the desire to create something new, unprecedented, something inherently sufficient.

What we need to do now, he said–always *in medias res*–is to bring the city and the novel together in a whole new manner. Dhaka's a new kind of city, a glimpse into our post-apocalyptic future, and it's time to find a form suitable to its reality. We were sitting in my store, which he had turned into his primary operating base. He stopped by, sometimes several times in a day: to leave his keys or pick up messages; to drop off parcels or laundry; to make phone calls or secure an abbreviated meal; to borrow cab fare or cigarette money, and then to return those puny hand loans and even to conduct complex, confusing arithmetic concerning these small exchanges. But, most importantly of all, he came by to hold his addas.

Bahar and Joydeep were regulars from the start. Bahar worked as a statistician for a research institute, but his heart, as with the rest of us, was sewn to literature. Joydeep was an anachronistic soul, and resisted any set occupation. Most of the others were students, or recent graduates, and many connected to some facet of the writing world: newspapers, publishing, little magazines, even copywriting in advertising firms. It was the spring after our first meeting, the start of a new millennium, and prophetic goals appeared to be in the realms of the possible again. Ramkamal held his addas, almost nightly, explaining to us the inevitability of this new codex. It will supply this city with a grammar, he said. It can't, sure as hell, be borrowed from places where the streetlights or plumbing work. What we need to write is nothing short of a manual. The Manual will explore how to be a citizen when the city itself is perpetually in deferral.

More than his ideas, at first, it was the verve with which he pursued them that affected us. And even more, his innovation lay in his ability to turn his personal mission into a collective enterprise. Everyone who entered his orbit was assigned a role. I was his keeper, in every sense. I kept his clothes and his cash—the erratic quantities that transected his days. And, increasingly, he started consigning to me his memories, unreliable as they were, and even more unreliably, his secrets. There were references, ever oblique, to his training in a Gandhi Village, before he turned sour on communes. Years spent as a distributor of East European farming machines. Visits as a functionary of a small-time Left party to Havana and Ho Chi Minh City.

It was hard to tell what was true and what he believed to be true. Once I even asked Shamsu, my friend in the Special Branch of police, if he could find out anything. These are not chaps who volunteer information easily. But we went a long way back, so he subjected me to a litany of standard queries: Has he taken money from you? Has he ever hit anyone? Does he keep the kind of company that worries you? Has anyone–since you met this guy–asked you for money? Suddenly, I felt bad that I'd asked Shamsu at all, and I prevaricated as much as I could to protect Ramkamal.

"If he's basically harmless, then why ask me to look into it at all?" Shamsu was a bit annoyed.

"Never mind," I said. "He just seemed like such an odd fellow, I just thought I'd ask."

Meantime, Ramkamal was all trust and exuberance. He was busy assigning jobs. Bahar, a brave and tireless sort, was his researcher. Joydeep, a sallow-faced depressive, was his typist and editor. Certain actors kept the role season after season, others for no longer than a few weeks. But, in any given moment, there was an entire cast to be filled: driver and bodyguard, handlers of bureaucratic affairs, minions to run petty personal errands, reporters to bring back news of events that he could not bear to attend, and sleuths to follow his enemies.

I was also expected to become his publisher. We never really talked about this obligation, let alone draft any contract to that end. To make such an assumption explicit on either side would have dishonored the deeper bonds of recognition that held us together ever since our first vodka-soaked encounter.

It seems odd now that I should have entertained Ramkamal to this extent. Most of his protégés were in their twenties. They were looking for a cause or movement to ennoble their eventless and unpromising lives. After many delays and futile anticipations, I had recently agreed to an arranged marriage with a seemingly sweet-natured girl, whose handsome forehead was marred by a splotch of discoloration roughly in the shape of England. I should have been immune to poetry in any form or disguise. Yet I had allowed Ramkamal to enter my life, and even to co-opt me to his purpose.

Not everyone in that bewitched circle knew the full extent of Ramkamal's dubious dealings, which started about a year after we met. Or perhaps they existed always, but were exposed to me only from the second year of our acquaintance. If I advised Ramkamal against keeping that kind of company, he'd say with a knowing smile, "You can't make money, real money, if you are not willing to trade with all kinds."

"You can also go to jail, if you do. You could even get mugged or killed," I told him.

"You worry too much, Burgher." That was the nickname he'd given me. "Worry will turn you into a dutiful citizen, increase your blood pressure. It will make you behave well with women, lose out on lucrative deals. Ultimately it will turn you into a bald little shopkeeper," said Ramkamal and guffawed in his booming voice.

Only Ramkamal could mock a person to his face without making them feel actually insulted. We were sitting in my store: me, on a high stool on my side of the counter and Ramkamal on another stool on his side. My cramped little store could barely hold Ramkamal. Why blame my store; the city could barely contain his personality.

That was possibly the other attraction of Ramkamal. It was thrilling to see someone defy the conventions of the city so thoroughly. Until Ramkamal came along, Dhaka to me was a gigantic composition in concrete, and a poor one at that. Nothing was well made, or quite in place. Tottering buildings stood on rickety pillars, paintjobs unfinished. Everything spilled over, jostled for an extra inch on the congested narrow roads. People left no room to breathe and exuded a noxious stink of sweat and avarice. The millions of them, despite their ceaseless movement, were ultimately letters affixed to the pages of a crude and merciless text.

I was no different. I lived in Kalabagan, and walked to my store on Mirpur Road every day by 10 am. According to Ramkamal, this little store of ours would become the radiant center of a new consciousness. Not like the bookselling hub of Aziz Supermarket, he said, and its pretenders with their long hair and their khadis, their ideologies and their grievances. We would write the great book of our times, the kind that had never been written before about Dhaka. It would ennoble this sweltering sewer of a city and in the process, rescue us as all. Rescue us from historical and literary anonymity.

At times there was a jarring contrast between Ramkamal and his rhetoric. One day, he turned up at my store wearing an approximation of a suit. Now that he was "in business," he announced, he had to dress "properly." This was well into the second year of our acquaintance, and this kind of swerve startled me less. Only in his mind could his outfit pass as proper business attire. A rumpled light green coat dangled off his broad but skeletal frame. Pants of a different shade stopped too far short of his ankles. The feet were still shod in his signature but much-faded red Keds. He was careful only with his hair, which at near-forty–an age no one knew for sure, but I deduced so from many dispersed clues– came down his nape in a lustrous flow.

"Better a living shopkeeper than dead anything," I said.

"That's where you're wrong, my friend. Better dead than the living dead," he replied.

"Why do the dead need money?" I said, not ready to relent.

"First, I'm neither dead, nor the living dead. I'm very much alive, and hence I have many needs. Second, I have accumulated debts of many kinds over the years, and some of the monetary ones need to be paid down. Some can't be paid back ever; they will be memorialized in my novel. Third, I need a cup of tea, if I am to continue your edification."

I called out to Chotka, who sat just outside, and did all the stacking, dusting, fetching. Chotka slept in the store at night and like an expert flycatcher, netted all the gossip that floated in the corridors of a building like ours. But even Chotka had been unable to capture any kernel of information from any quarter to aid the search for Ramkamal.

"Tell me something, Ramkamal. Do you have any rent to pay?"

"No, not in the conventional sense," he replied.

"How about your meals? Do they come mostly for free?"

"I have been blessed in my friendships," he admitted.

"What other expenses do you have? This suit of yours, isn't it borrowed?" I asked, pointing at his garment. "And by the looks of it, borrowed from several different parties."

"I do my best not to stress any single benefactor," responded Ramkamal in his faux-docile mode.

"Then, why do you need money, Ramkamal?"

"It is astonishing how much you don't understand, Burgher," said Ramkamal, raising to his lips the small, dirty, steaming cup that Chotka had brought around with extra haste. What you don't understand, Ramkamal told me that day, reverting to the professorial mode that came to him so naturally and to which the rest of us submitted as if by hypnosis, is this: The attempt to live a life free of cost is actually more time consuming than earning the costs you're trying to avoid. You see, when you don't pay and others are keeping you as a favor, you too end up doing favors for them. They may not expect it of you, not explicitly, and even you might not think quid pro quo, but an exchange of indirect equivalencies must transpire. A woman lets you stay in her guest room, you end up helping her children with homework. Or you sit around after dinner gabbing with the dotard of a husband, so that no domestic harmonies are ruffled on your account. Do you have any idea how many hours you lose in the process? To say nothing of the energy! Nothing drains you more than the undeserving. To entertain them, let alone the folly of trying to educate them, you might as well try to grow aubergines in the desert. And I have been doing that all my life. Now time is running out. I will need at least ten years to finish The Manual. I need to make enough money to get away for ten years. I need to make that kind of money as fast as I can. I have so little time, said Ramkamal, staring at his palm, as if he could see the future in it.

"Take a sabbatical. You know I'll pay for it. But stop these dealings," I said.

"How long can you put me up, Burgher? I need ten years," said Ramkamal.

"It's a collective project," I said, feeling a bit irritated and defiant. "Why should it take so long?"

"I'm collectivizing the project precisely because I don't think I have time. So, it will go on, even if I can't. Besides, I don't want to think of it as a finite project. It should go on as long as the city endures. It should expand and change, old volumes should be re-issued with sections appropriately revised. Let it be a living document."

There was an impenetrable circularity, and completeness, to his logic that was hard to contest. He could rebuff uncommonly generous offers, without a thank you, while the benefactor felt small for failing to come up with the extent of support actually required by him. Still, I did not take any offense. I believed in Ramkamal and shared his tribal faith in the magic of the printed word: any place, once sufficiently expressed in letters, becomes transformed. In fact, until that happens, the place doesn't really exist. Everything about Dhaka that undermined us—the mulish toil of rickshaw-pullers, pot-holed roads, betel-spitting pedestrians over-loud billboards, faux-marble facades, the sheer mindless quantity of shoddy products in the countless stores, and the limitless gluttony of their victims—all this would be conferred a halo of unforeseen meaning once Ramkamal's work was complete.

Ramkamal brought us samples, periodically, of the ultimate revelation. Some of them were too obscure even for our circle—one piece began with the cryptic sentence, "After the experiments were over, one brain remained"—and others displayed sheer virtuosity of organization. The book was going to be an encyclopedia of the city, its neighborhoods and the corresponding human types, which to him were interrelated, though not interchangeable. Each type was illustrated by one or more specific characters, but with a vividness and accuracy of condemnation that held nothing back. The section on "Personalities" was indexed and cross-referenced to other ones: "Sites," "Follies," "Precedents: Historical," and so on.

The arrival of each new section or its additions, constituted an event in our little world. News of the readings was carefully guarded by the initiated. By then we shared Ramkamal's paranoia to an extent that we took the trouble of making a show of closing the store for the evening and then gathering again past midnight, shutters drawn, to keep any interlopers at bay and to imbibe the latest installment undisturbed. Sometimes Ramkamal read out the new parts slowly in his sonorous baritone. Other times, he'd ask a favorite to read it out, while he took long, slow, drags on his cheap cigarettes–the only one whom I could not forbid, even when the vestibule was sealed–watching our expressions with a smile that was both parental in its joy at making a gift and childlike in its eager anticipation of praise. I have lived no purer moments in this life. Even Chotka, who understood not a word, would stand through these recitations, leaning his slight body against the drawn shutters, clearly in a state of rapture.

"You see, you see, Burgher?" Ramkamal would ask me half chidingly the following day. "It's beginning. We are going to endow the primitive brain of this city with a cortex."

Ramkamal was not content, however, only to assign the reading of his pieces to his followers. He conscripted them into the writing as well. "I can never write such a vast, in fact endless, tract by myself," he told us. "You have to do your parts, each one of you."

"What can we do? This is your book," Bahar had said, the first time Ramkamal floated this idea of a collective authorship.

"It's our book, and we will all write it," said Ramkamal.

"How can we all write it, Kamal-da? Not all of us can write, and the few who can, not as well as you," said Joydeep.

"You write well enough, and you will get better at it. I will show you," said Ramkamal.

"It'll never sound like you," Joydeep persisted.

"Presto! That is the point. We will write the first multi-tonal novel. How can you write about a city in a single voice?"

"And the ones who can't write?" Bahar queried.

"If you can't write, you will research. If you can't do either, you'll bring back photos, sounds, news. You will help take care of logistics and security, keep us safe from the clowns and serpents. There is a role for everyone, no matter how indirect."

That was how the project became collectivized. But doing research for Ramkamal wasn't easy. There was no telling what he'd want to know: What kind of currency did the Armenians use when they first arrived in Dhaka? When was modern plumbing first put into this city? What is the size of the monkey population in Bongaon today?

Writing for Ramkamal was even harder: drafts were sent back with virtually every sentence marked with a blue pencil, and it took up to dozen or more versions for a literary amanuensis to reach a copy where only a few words would be circled.

Then one day he'd ask someone to ferry tightly wrapped, heavy crates of rattling bottles from a warehouse in Uttara to various hotels around town. If the protégé were naïve enough to ask how this task was related to the book, he'd say, "Never doubt the mission. Never doubt the mentor."

As the oldest, most experienced one of that crowd, I should have probably been more skeptical. Yet, every time I felt any questions arising inside me about Ramkamal's ways, if not his talent or his intents, he'd arrive with a fresh section: "Crimes, or Livelihood," "Correspondences: Literary," "Graveyards, Ghats, etc."–offering a whole new way of looking at persons or topics covered before from a different angle in other sections, and adding new layers to their story. The narrative, and the suspense–not only of its contents but also the manner of its unfolding–were too good to give up on Ramkamal.

By last winter, we knew that we had accumulated no less than a few hundred pages of this masterpiece. But, I could see no end in sight. It could go on for years, for thousands of pages. The project was designed to be endless, Ramkamal boasted. At what point then do we share it with the world? I wondered.

"You will know when the story has reached its first great inflection point," said Ramkamal, freely introducing a new terminology, without bothering to explain it. "We will share it in pieces, that lack of finality and anticipation will protect it."

The only thing I could see reaching an inflection point—assuming I'd understood the term correctly—was Ramkamal himself. For the first time since we met, he appeared a bit preoccupied and at times even forlorn. He even came to the store a little less often. The changes were subtle enough that only a daily observer like me would notice.

"Can you loan me some money?"

God knew Ramkamal owed me lacs already in various forms: rent, food, clothes, taxi rides, bribes for official works, gifts for people who had to be entertained, tuition or medical help for people who deserved it—the list went on. He never took the payment himself; it was always given to one of his lackeys, and they'd run it over to the beneficiary or the vendor or the creditor directly.

"You've never asked me for money before," I said, meaning that he'd never borrowed any substantial amount of cash till then.

"I will return it within a week, of course," he said.

I knew it was pointless to ask him why he needed the money. I asked how much, and although the sum was larger than I expected, I could count it out from my till. It was winter, my favorite time of the year. I liked nothing better than to watch a heavy cloak of fog descend on Dhaka streets. The colder the days, thicker the fog, the more I enjoyed it. I liked the appearance, anomalous for Dhaka streets, of heavily-dressed office-goers and cars with headlights turned on in daytime. It was a particularly cold winter, yet I refused to let anyone pull the shutter down all the way. I brought in a space-heater and told everyone to wear more layers. Ramkamal had stopped writing. He told us, "I've decided, I won't write in winters anymore."

"Why?" The befuddled audience gasped in unison.

"There is a time to write and a time to withdraw, to purify," he said.

"So, what shall we do in winter?"

"We shall converse," he declaimed.

Everyone was stunned by this announcement. But, no one knew what to tell Ramkamal. One day Bahar and Joydeep, Ramkamal's two most steadfast devotees, came to me together. "Kamalda's not quite himself," they said.

"That's how geniuses are," I said, not entirely convinced myself. "They can be moody and unpredictable."

"How do you know?" Joydeep asked. "Have you met a genius before?"

Joydeep was the most intelligent of the apprentices. The only one who possessed both the intelligence and the verbal felicity to continue the project, if one had to do so without the guidance of Ramkamal. But he was also a sour fellow, as much due to poor digestion, I suspected, as on account of an overgrown sense of skepticism.

"No, that's just what people say," I replied feebly, and said nothing about my recent loan to Ramkamal, which he had not returned in a month. Bahar and Joydeep were not the only people to register a concern about Ramkamal. More disquietingly, a week later Shamsu, the SB official, came to see me. He sat on Ramkamal's stool and chucked handfuls of peanut into his maw with unfailing accuracy. He nattered on about the misfortunes of a friend, who on becoming richer than us, rarely responded to our calls anymore. "But the minute the motherfucker gets into trouble, who does he call?" And Shamsu's broad face, always so tense as if he were challenging the world to a duel, broke into a wide and vindicated grin. "Oh, I make him sweat for these favors, don't you worry."

I didn't worry; I was well aware of Shamsu's capacity for misanthropy. But, we tend to have a strange tolerance for people we know from childhood, no matter how poorly they turned out. I wondered if Shamsu felt the same way about me. Certainly, he felt that way about almost everyone we knew in common. But what concerned me more on that day was his renewed interest in Ramkamal.

"How well do you know this chap?" he asked.

"I see him almost every day," I said, feeling defensive again.

"Which says nothing about how well you know him," he replied. He knew how to hold a silence, when someone was being intractable.

"He's a character. You know how writers tend to be. No telling where he'll sleep or eat, lives almost day to day."

"Look, it's none of my concern, but you're an old friend, and a good friend, that's why I asked," said Shamsu.

"Why, have you heard something?"

"In my line of work, we hear so many things. But, I can't trust anything, unless we've done a real investigation, and everything that doesn't go into the final report is usually true."

"There is an investigation?"

"Oh no, nothing like that yet. But, his name, or people he knows, their names come up now and then."

Shamsu didn't say more that day. If I were a more anxious type, though, just that much from an SB Inspector might have been enough to unsettle me. For a few days I felt a bit wary. Ramkamal seemed to pick up on that too, but said nothing. For a while he even reduced his visits to my store. Then one day I heard that Bahar was down with jaundice. I went to visit him in Goran—an area I never visited otherwise—with a basket of fruits. Ramkamal was there already, and had moved full-time into Bahar's hostel to take care of the boy. For a full month, Ramkamal gave up virtually all his other activities. I felt a little bad about harboring any doubts about a man who could give himself so unstintingly to his putative family.

We were being too hard on Ramkamal, I told Joydeep, who concurred. We pointed out to each other what else Ramkamal did for people. He could make uncanny predictions and gave hope to the hopeless. He tutored boys who despaired of passing the Civil Service Exam—for free—and with results. For girls who wanted to marry the boy of their choice, Ramkamal would arrange the Qazi to officiate the union, the getaway, the honeymoon, and even the subsequent mitigation with the family. People who needed to evade loan sharks or stave off small-time extortionists, they sought out Ramkamal. Petty functionaries of the government, who sought promotions, even they came to him for advice.

He did not offer all kinds of help at any given moment. This kind of work takes a very special kind of concentration, he explained. During the last winter of our acquaintance, he was focused on visas to obscure destinations—countries in Central Europe and sub-Saharan Africa. This was a new line for him, and it started, as with so many of his endeavors, he told me penitently, by simply agreeing to fill out forms. You know to what lengths I go to avoid them, said Ramkamal. This was true and this was why he could never rent a place for himself or open a bank account. But I can't say no to others. And one thing always leads to the next. Take me to the interview, Kamal-da, please! On one occasion, he even stood for the applicant at the interview. These second-rate countries have such lax standards you know, he said.

"Is this safe? Is this really necessary?" I asked him.

"All this, you see, is ultimately in the service of The Manual," he said. "I can't write, if I can't get free first. I must get free from all these obligations...I need a place, paid for, and a caretaker who will bring me food three times a day and never start a conversation. Once I get to that place, perhaps in the hills, or by the sea, or in a small town, but some place where I will be free from situations and the curious, indeed free too from my own curiosity, once I get there, I can begin to write."

Although I had neither the talent nor the hankering to write, this was a longing I could understand. This was the Ramkamal we all still loved and wanted to rescue. This was the Ramkamal who still held addas. In fact, he had become more regular about those evening sessions ever since he stopped writing. It was time, he said, for us to understand the real comedy hidden in the peregrinations of a Don Quixote or a Leopold Bloom. He commissioned readings like a professor who believes nothing but his subject is of importance to the student. But unlike the hacks at the university, Ramkamal actually taught us something. He introduced us to the dark terrors of a Kafka and to the charms of a Von Kleist. It was Ramkamal who taught us to appreciate the dyspepsia of a Bernhard and the mysticism of a Kis. He was utterly unapologetic about his partiality to the Europeans. He was willing to make exceptions for "necessary" Americans, especially from the South—Carpentier and Cortazar, Borges and Rulfo, and a retinue of other magicians. He made exceptions similarly for other figures from the fringe—the Kadares and the Goytisolos—who had managed by the force of their unique visions and literary execution to rise to a level of universal relevancy, but in his esteem virtually no Bengali made the cut. Any newcomer to his sessions, who pestered him too much on that point, trotting out Bengali sentimentalists and socialists alike for approval, would be held in a protracted gray gaze. The faint-hearted deserted our camp; the survivors became regulars. No one was allowed to take any written notes. People stop listening when they start to write, he said. The adda was held always late at night when no ordinary shoppers came. We borrowed stools from the neighboring stores, and Chotka fetched countless rounds of tea from the stall in the side alley. In his final sessions, Ramkamal extolled hidden gems like di Lampedusa's *The Leopard* and Marai's *Embers*.

No, there was no denying Ramkamal, or his passion. No doubting his talents or his know-how, his sheer vitality. But now that nine months have elapsed, we need to reconsider the episode of Ramkamal. The end of it came, the way these things do, not in a cataclysmic single event, but in a succession of non-events. First, there was the week of sessions with no Ramkamal, when the puzzled disciples stared at each other questioningly. With a person like Ramkamal, when you don't see him for a few days, you think someone else will know where he is. He must be on one of his escapades. Once the queries became circular, slowly it dawned on us that no one knew his whereabouts, and then the protégés fanned out all over the city.

A few of them got concerned immediately about the small amounts owed to them by Ramkamal. Yet others became consumed with worry. They checked all the houses where Ramkamal was known to have been a guest or even visitor. They checked the odd venues where he was known to have spent his nights: a warehouse and a massage-parlor, both in Uttara; the ante-room of a doctor's chambers on Elephant Road; the upstairs of a restaurant in Sadar Ghat. Places I never knew Ramkamal frequented. Once the initial reports were all in–or, shall we say, reached an inflection point?–the pack of learners broke into a schism.

The doubters were quick and ferocious in their judgment: We knew all along the man was a fraud. He took us around all over town on fool's errands. He took our money. And what did he leave us in return? Just these worthless pages. They don't even make any sense. The doubters were led by Bahar, whom until then I'd thought to be the deepest of the believers. A number of the defectors, even total strangers, filed cases against me, citing documents that bore signatures vaguely resembling mine. Apparently, I was an accomplice to Ramkamal's perfidies.

The believers countered: You don't know that he ran away. You don't know if he hasn't met some grievous end. And don't forget, he gave away more than any amount he took from any of us. How can you be so ungrateful to a teacher like him? What do you know, that's worth knowing, that you didn't learn from him?

I did not participate in these quarrels. I talked to a lawyer about the cases and then went to see Shamsu. He had been transferred to some special unit with new offices in Agargaon. The building, as with so many Dhaka edifices, was of course unfinished and gave off the strong chemical reek of new paint. But Shamsu appeared highly content behind his enormous desk. I wondered if government officers required such wide platforms as a kind of rampart between themselves and their visitors.

"So, it's about Ramkamal?"

I did not grudge him this bit of self-satisfaction, and at least with me he possessed the kindness not to drag it out.

"I can't say we have any definite information either," said Shamsu. "You see, no one's filed a missing person report, and the cases against him–alleged fraud, swindling, loan-default–all that's not going to go anywhere. Even the people filing the cases know that. But, there's nothing in his track record that's heavy enough for us to take any active interest. We are rather interested in a few of the people he fell in with–not you, or your funny circle of bookworms–but others that I suspect you knew little about. But even with them, his connection was not clear or sustained enough for us to really turn him into a subject."

"Is there nothing else you can tell me?"

"I could, but it won't be anything that helps you find him," said Shamsu. "I suspect he's gone for good."

I found Shamsu's bluntness helpful. A peon brought us two cups of tea. Shamsu was high up enough now that instead of serving bad tea by itself, he could serve it with bad condensed milk. But, as I sipped that horrid tea and watched the sun slope down the western sky—"see for you it's the first time, but we see all types"—I barely heard Shamsu anymore. I felt as if I were awakening from a dream. Although, many of the hopefuls still think that Ramkamal will magically appear again one day, I know that the magic we experienced with him the first time around can never be recreated, not even by him. I am increasingly sure that we may never see him again, and I am also secretly glad that that is the case.

On the first anniversary of Ramkamal's disappearance, I celebrated the expansion of my store. My bookshelves, much expanded, boast literature from all corners of the world, even Bengali—but in a secret tribute to Ramkamal, no Tagore novels. I took over the space next door, and put in four square tables to start a small café—and new addas. Chotka became the manager of this café. I harbored no grand nor definite expectations of the new adda. It was not for me, but for a new generation. Everyone had to find their own way to live the Manual. Joydeep kept the Manual itself alive, by adding new pages to it, even entire new sections. Rumor had it, splintered elements from our crew were composing their versions of the Manual. It wouldn't matter who came out with one first, or who finally succeeded, if anyone, at capturing even a shade of Ramkamal's vision. I was pretty sure that he'd be quite happy, if he knew—and sometimes, sitting alone in my store, late at night, I couldn't shake the feeling that he was out there somewhere and that he did know—that the Manual was alive. Not just in the form of texts but as a living guide, indeed, a pulsating document inside each of us, of how to be vital in a world without letters.

Elephant Road

Aninda could not understand why he did what he did on Elephant Road. It was true that Bangladesh had completely thrown away a series-winning match against Zimbabwe the night before. He was also fired from his job of twelve years that morning. But nothing could explain what he did.

Aninda had trudged over to that congested shop-filled street, where the buildings jostled shoulder to shoulder as densely as the pedestrians milling in their shadows, to buy a pair of PT shoes for his daughter. No need for the girl to go without new shoes one more day, he reasoned, just because I lost my job. Besides, he needed to digest the news by himself first.

"We have found severe discrepancies in the bank reconciliations," Aninda was sternly informed by the young son of the boss. Truth be told, Aninda did not enjoy his place of work anymore. He liked it in the easy-going days of the big boss, when they could enjoy long afternoons of free papers and endless cups of tea. Then came the boss' son, and with him arrived an insufferable regime of software and audits, meetings and agenda.

Aninda cursed himself for not having quit before they had a chance to fire him. It wasn't as if he had nothing else to fall back on. He had put up a store of his own a few years ago, looked after by his wife's brother. But a regular paycheck was a hard habit to kick.

When he walked out of the office, for what he fancied might be the last time ever, he decided to head for his favorite restaurant at Shahbagh, at the top of Elephant Road. The shoe store would be close enough afterwards. He stared out the second-floor window, comfortable in his air-conditioned perch, and tried to judge by their looks if any of the passersby were also fired that day.

At 4 o'clock Aninda stepped out of the restaurant and headed for the corner that the Bata shoe store had occupied for decades. He picked out a pair of blue PT shoes – the kind with two white stripes and strong rubber soles. They would go well with his daughter's uniform, and also hopefully hold out longer than the last pair. When he walked out of the store, suddenly he heard a cry rise from the crowd, "Catch him! Catch him!"

Aninda did not even hear clearly what the crowd was shouting. Aninda could not see anything that looked like a crowd. Just the usual jostle of people, and wending through them, with cheetah-like swiftness, a young man with a half-open shirt and eyes wide with terror. Then he saw the chasers, also young, eyes full of rage, fingers pointing, hair flying, spearing through the pedestrians. "Catch him! Catch him!"

From the time Aninda spotted the quarry, it took barely a second for the boy to reach him. Perhaps Aninda would have acted differently if he had even a few more seconds to think, he told himself later. But, in that moment, he let the bag slip down his arm to free his hands, grabbed onto the light pole before him with both arms and stuck a foot out, catching the boy at the shin.

The boy didn't fall down outright, but he stumbled. A moment's slowdown was all the mob needed. As he grabbed at air to maintain balance, someone thrust him flat to the ground with one push. He had no chance of getting up.

Someone slapped Aninda on the back, "Well done!" A crowd swelled in no time around the boy's fallen figure. Aninda could hear the curses, harsh like clashing metal. And below the shouting voices, he could hear the sickeningly muted slap of flesh on flesh.

Aninda pulled back into the crowd quietly and then decided to walk away before anyone noticed him. He hoped that they would not kill the boy. He hoped that the boy was guilty of something. He expected to read about him in the papers the next day.

When Aninda came home, still trembling from the incident, he found his wife's brother Nitun at the dining table. The brother was a cause for merry distraction for his wife, and Aninda could slip into his room without attention or comment. Aninda took a bath with cold bucket-water, pouring countless mugs over his head. But the boy he tripped, his terrified gaunt face refused to be washed out of his memory.

"Don't use up all the water," his wife shouted with a rap on the door. When he finally emerged, he found Nitun with a cup of tea and the remains of four person's worth of fried chicken on an enamel plate. The dining table was squeezed into a tiny square between the kitchen and the living area. Except when Aninda watched cricket, their daughter kept possession of the TV. The adults took their tea at the table, feeling the heat of the stove through the open kitchen door.

"I was telling Didi, brother, that what we need is a children's corner," said Nitun with a clever look as if he was about to tell a secret. "You see, if the mothers have a place to dump their kids, why will they go to another shop? Think about it, brother. It's a genius strategy."

Aninda hated it when Nitun called him "brother" in English. Aninda hated it too when Nitun used words like "genius" or "strategy." Nitun belonged to a new generation, which did not believe in degrees or toil. They gelled their hair into porcupine spikes, sported neon-bright sneakers, and carried mobile phones that rang out theme songs from movies Aninda would never see.

"Haven't I told you not to wear such tight T-shirts?" Aninda said, ignoring Nitun's business idea altogether.

"Why, what's wrong with it?" The boy asked with cheery exclamation. "It's Hugo Boss, original!"

"I can see your nipples, that's what's wrong with the shirt."

"You are so conservative, brother. Tight is the fashion."

"Are nipple displays also in fashion?" I hate men with breasts, thought Aninda. Maybe it was Nitun that he really hated, but he could not identify any justifiable cause for such antipathy, and so did not allow the thought to become a conscious awareness.

"Why don't you stop picking on him and listen to his ideas for a moment?" Aninda's wife intervened, as she planted a steaming dish of mutton on the placemat.

"What do I need to listen to his ideas for? I just need to see if the numbers add up," Aninda said grimly.

"Numbers will get better, brother, if you listen to my ideas," said Nitun. "We need more space to put in a children's corner. I think the guys next door are looking to sell."

He is not daunted by me at all anymore, thought Aninda edgily. This is not good. I have to start sitting at the cash counter myself if I am to see profits. This boy with his gelled hair and pointy nipples will ruin me. I must curb him before he can strike out on his own.

"Why don't you give him some share of the profits?" Aninda's wife asked him, as she undressed for the night. Profits? Was this her idea, or was it Nitun ventriloquizing through his sister?

"You know, he's getting older. He's thinking about marrying. How long can he go just on salary?"

"Who will marry him?" Aninda protested. "He has breasts. Women don't need men with breasts, they have their own."

"Stop being so mean," said his wife with a chuckle. "There's nothing wrong with how Nitun looks."

Aninda was content to have deflected the issue for the moment. This was the first time his wife had raised the issue of giving her brother a stake in the business, and he knew it would not be the last. A new epicenter of anxiety had just been introduced into his cheerless life. The worry pulled him out of bed into the tiny verandah adjoining his bedroom in the middle of the night. He thought of his lost job, of Nitun, and then the boy he had tripped. He sat in a stupor overlooking a neighbor's unkempt garden. A craggy guava tree confronted him like a question mark in the soft glow of a half moon.

Why could he not simply recount the incident to his wife? He didn't exactly feel guilty or ashamed, yet he felt his gorge pushing up every time he thought of the moment and the gleeful ferocity of the fast forming mob. No, there was no name, he was certain, in any known lexicon for what he felt. Regret, perhaps, was the closest kin to this emotion, but there was no confirmation forthcoming from the guava tree, his only audience.

Aninda felt a strange tremor in his limbs when he awoke the next morning, but could not tell if it was from the incident still or just from lack of sleep. After dropping his daughter off at school, he bought the five papers they kept in his office and took them to Ramna Park. He had never been a park lover, but he did not know where else to go. Cafes and restaurants cost money. He found a shady bench and scanned every inch of each paper in futile search for news of the boy.

Three days passed, and every morning Aninda dutifully knotted a tie as if going to work. The tremors subsided but did not disappear, and he could not shake off the vision of the boy from his mind. On the fourth day after the event, frustrated by the papers, Aninda went back to the Bata store. The salesman who had sold him the PT shoes proved chatty and recounted the incident with elaborate details at the slightest prompting. Aninda learned from him that the hijacker—as the salesman described the boy—was rescued from the mob by the police and possibly at the Dhaka Medical College Hospital in police custody.

Aninda bought a half dozen oranges on his way to the hospital. A small tip to a cleaner led him to the ward where the boy was held. The ward was a vast high-ceilinged room of Great War gloom. The walls were mapped with peeling paint and colorful stains. The beds, ancient iron ships, were covered with loosely tucked, dirty, yellowed linen. The patients were grateful to have a bed though, and their hopeless well-wishers sat by their sides with gaunt worried faces.

The boy was in a corner bed near the entrance to the ward. One arm was hooked to a saline drip, the other cuffed to the iron rods of his bedpost. Aninda pulled up a white wooden stool. The boy was fast asleep, the cage of his narrow bony chest rising and falling in deep and steady rhythms. He was still wearing the checkered green-white shirt in which the mob had captured him, but now it was torn in a couple of places. A bandage was wrapped around the boy's head. A brownish seepage marked it in places.

What am I doing here? Aninda asked himself. And while he could think of no good answer, he also could not remove himself from the scene. A half hour after Aninda's arrival the boy opened his eyes, and seeing the stranger he asked, "What do you want?"

"I was there when it happened, brother," Aninda said. When the boy asked if he was a reporter, Aninda acquiesced to the role.

"I wanted to hear your side of the story," Aninda said, getting off his bed. "You know how the papers are. Any hijacking gets three lines in the city page. I want to understand the entire phenomenon. Where you come from, where they come from," Aninda said, surprised by the fluency of his inventions.

Aninda stayed until dusk during that first conversation. The boy's eyes, heavy-lidded from torpor and drugs, brightened a little as they talked. The boy came from a small district town in the south. His father was a teacher and thought that his son worked in a trading company. "Not untrue, in a manner of speaking," added the boy with a chuckle. He had three siblings; the oldest had gone abroad illegally–Italy–and sent them little money, and even that irregularly. The younger two, a boy and a girl, were both still in school.

There was nothing uncommon in the boy's story. Aninda did not find out everything about him on that first visit, but he came the next day, and the next, with a notepad, jotting down everything the boy had to say. He held a series of odd jobs in the city, as a peon and as a store clerk. But the pace of advancement in these positions was too slow for his appetites. He wanted to wear branded jeans and to live in a better building. Where he stayed now, the floor flooded at the first splash of rain. He wanted cable TV and someday a motorbike.

By the fourth visit, a week after their first meeting, there was little left to learn about the boy. At least, in his capacity as a reporter. Aninda felt the interviews had helped to develop a certain bond between the two of them. The boy saw him as a man of rare kindness and clearly welcomed his visits. Apparently, his boss was the only other person who had visited him during this time. The boss had secured a bail for him, and the handcuffs were gone.

"They'll let me go in two days," said the boy. "And as soon as this cast is off," he said raising his right arm, "I'll be back to full duty."

"Really, do you want to go back to that? After what happened?"

"My boss is a good man. I owe it to him," said the boy solemnly. "Anyway, don't worry, we'll be in touch. You are like a brother now. Anyone gives you any trouble, you just give me one ring, and I'll be there."

Nitun's face flashed before Aninda's eyes for a second. Nitun had dared asked him directly for a cut of the profits. Brother and sister were ganging up on him together. He felt squeezed smaller every day by an invisible vise.

Aninda had caught himself in recent days in passing reveries in which the boy roughed up Nitun for him. Aninda had also given passing thought to the notion of firing Nitun and employing the boy instead. He wanted to do something for the boy. He didn't know what else to do with his guilt or remorse or whatever strange compulsion had driven him to form this peculiar rapport with his victim.

Aninda was a little disturbed however to hear how eager the boy was to get back to his work. The job he could have offered him suddenly seemed like a no-match for what the boy already had. There was not much else Aninda had to offer, except the confession. He had already balked at it for a week; there would be no better time for it.

"You know, it is so strange that we get along so well," said Aninda, "if you think of how we came together."

"In your line of work, I'm sure you meet all sorts of people," said the boy. And then with a chuckle, he added, "So do I!"

"This is not where we first met," said Aninda, looking straight into the boy's eyes. "I am not really a reporter. I am the man who tripped you up on Elephant Road."

The boy looked at him blankly, as if unable to comprehend the meaning of the statement just offered to him.

"I know this will come as a shock to you," Aninda added. "Please understand that I didn't really mean to hurt you. I don't know how it happened."

The boy was now sitting up in disbelief. "Is this a joke, you filthy sister-fucking mongrel? Why did you come here? To see the damage you had caused? To see what good work you had done, you son-of-a-whore?"

"Call me what you will, brother," Aninda said in a suppressed voice, "I know I deserve it." Aninda could feel his heart pounding, but he held a calm exterior. "Please know that I meant no harm, it was an accident. That's why I came to see you, to say sorry, to see if I could help. Can't you forgive me?"

"Forgive you? Why? So you can feel good about yourself, you shit-eater? I had already forgiven the man who had tripped me, even the men who beat me. I will not forgive someone who comes to toy with me. You will pay for this," said the boy, now at the top of his voice, his face red from anger and exertion.

Aninda stood up, and the other patients in the ward also sat up in their beds in alarm. Aninda took a step towards the boy, but before he could complete it the boy leaned forward and spit a thick gob of yellow mucus into his face. Aninda jumped back, and the boy too tried to swing himself out of bed. Luckily, he was in a tangle of sheets. And there was the drip. He cursed Aninda non-stop, while struggling to extricate the needle from his arm that tethered him to the saline drip.

Aninda took this momentary delay to gain a lead on the boy. He ran out of the ward into the corridor, pausing for a fraction at the door, to hurl a final apology over his shoulder, "Forgive me, I didn't mean any of it," and then flew full speed towards the stairs. As he fled he could hear the boy's voice exploding expletives behind his back.

A nurse was already entering the ward and shouting at someone behind her to hurry up. Heads poked out of other doorways at this commotion. The boy was held back by two nurses, and surrounded by a gaggle of observers—patients in pajamas, visitors, hospital staff.

Aninda took one last look at the boy from the distance before bounding down the stairs three steps at a time.

When Aninda was out on the street, he kept looking over his shoulder and moved at a jaunty pace. When he had turned the corner onto another street and lost himself in a throng of hundreds of men, men who looked alike and filled the Dhaka streets with no evident purpose, he felt finally safe.

"I'll find you, I'll find you," was the last threat hurled at his back by the boy. Aninda was glad that he had told the boy that he lived in Old Town, miles in the opposite direction from Uttara, where he actually lived. That was also where his store was located, far away from the areas where the boy usually worked. For the first time in years, Aninda felt thankful for the vastness of the city and the congestion of the millions of idle men among whom he could hide.

That evening Aninda finally told his wife that he had lost his job. Although, when he told her, he said that it had happened only the day before. Since he had received his final settlement the previous day, the fat check seemed to mitigate the blow. Instead of blaming him, his wife became indignant on his behalf.

"People will use you till the moment they don't need you and then chuck you like a sucked-out bone."

It was not often that Aninda and his wife agreed. It was less often that she took his side. Or so he felt. So he basked in the warm, soothing glow of her indignation.

"What do you want to do now?" She asked him finally. "Surely, someone will want an experienced accountant like you?"

Her hopefulness, or estimation of his worth, was touching. Nothing depressed him like misplaced hope. They sat at the dining table, with the remains of a special chicken curry his wife made with tomatoes. For a flash, he could see vividly how she looked the first year of their marriage, a face completely unscarred by illness, by time. He did not want to mislead her on this issue any longer.

"I don't think I'll look for another job. I'm going to expand the store," said Aninda.

"Business? Wouldn't it be good to have a steady income from somewhere?"

Aninda told his wife that in this age of ever smarter candidates, he could not land any job that would be worth having.

"Nitun has been dying to expand the store anyway, so why not now?" he said.

"He will be so happy," said his wife. "You really should give him a share though."

"I'll think about it," said Aninda.

After their daughter was put to bed in her small room, or rather an abutment off the living room, they sat in the sofa with cardamom tea. They used to have this tea every night in the first year of their marriage. It was also a time when they used to talk often of the life ahead. The talks ceased unnoticed. But tonight they talked again, about the store and the future, everything that they would be able to do with the money they made.

Aninda was up again, however, long after his wife fell asleep. Not because he felt upset, as he had almost every night for the past week. For once, pressures and anxieties receded. A feeling of being restored suffused him. He watched over the tiny garden, enclosed by towering apartment blocks. He knew that this accidental sanctuary too might disappear one day. But it was here now and all to himself. The strange guava tree, looking like an old man on this moonlit night, kept him company, and for once that was enough.

All My Enemies

Shahbaz kept his whole morning, and half the office, busy with details of the celebrations that night. The flowers, the flowers! He wanted fresh orchids flown in from Bangkok. And the chairs draped in silky blue material, not the usual white cotton shit. And none of the cheap fairy lighting either. Frightened staff nodded and rushed off to make phone calls. We want pixels of starry white light defining the contours of the garden and the hedges. Shahbaz was turning sixty, and he felt sad that he could find no one but himself to organize the party.

One would have expected his family to arrange the event. But that was not his situation. He loved his wife: a sweet and devoted soul, but utterly unable to organize anything, and absolutely no good with details. Belkis suffered from headaches and depression and other ailments that he could hardly keep track of. She maintained a ritual of prayers and cures so elaborate that Shahbaz did not dare coordinate other operations with her daily system. She was best left alone. Even if she could not organize the party, she would turn out for it, that much he could count on. And when she did, even after all these years, she would still manage somehow to look stunning.

The children were no better, perhaps worse.

The daughter, once so lithe and vivacious, proved good only at losing husbands. Twice by the age of thirty! And not a child from one of them! Sonya blamed them, her parents, for the first divorce, as the marriage was arranged by them. So Shahbaz let her pick the second husband, and she picked a cripple. It was one of those moments when Shahbaz could say nothing. Who, in this day and age, is allowed to speak against a cripple? Not that that was the primary cause of his objection. But, having managed people all his life, he could smell a skunk from a distance, no matter how well disguised. And sure enough, within a year of marriage, she came home early one day from a canceled lunch to discover the day-nurse bobbing on her cripple's lap in the center of the drawing room.

Since she moved back, she had gained almost a dozen kilos.

The son, Imtiaz, a chicken-necked coward, too tall for any purpose, hid behind his books and cameras and spouted philosophy in response to every practical exigency. So much for a Yale education! When the boy graduated and came home a year back, Shahbaz got his hopes up. Finally, he might have an ally in his long, lonely battle. A protégé, a successor, a person in whom he could confide everything. Instead, the boy spent all his time filming peddlers of vanishing trades, street kids, lowlifes. This fascination with the poor disturbed Shahbaz and so did Imtiaz's friends: the boys and girls looking alike in virtuous uniforms of khadi kurtas and long hair.

"Give him some time," said Belkis, ever tolerant of the world and its blemishes. "Let him settle down a bit."

With a family like that, Shahbaz preferred to rely on himself. He had in fact relied– his entire life– only on himself. His father, a man full of the goodness of incompetence, was no support. No relatives to give him a lift at any stage–it was all him and few rare mentors and allies that luck had thrown his way in rare fits of mercy.

Shahbaz stood up from his humongous black desk for a stretch. He kept an exceedingly clean office. It took up almost the entire forty-first floor, the highest in the city, not just in his building. He had finished this tower, his magnum opus, only the previous year. The view from his office, commanding three directions–East, South and West–gave him a deep sense of completion. Before him lay the conquered city, behind him the scabrous northern edge, just ripe for expansion.

He walked across the gray marble floor to the edge of the room. The floor-to-ceiling window caught a light reflection of him: a head still full of wavy back-brushed hair. The lines on his face were obscured by the tinted surface of the heavy glass. What he focused on though were new towers coming up in the distance. Sometimes he used a pair of binoculars to survey his prey. A building had to sit unfinished only so long before he knew he could swoop down to pick it up on the cheap.

The city boasted a hundred properties, if not more, with his name emblazoned on their facades. Why did he build all this? What purpose did it serve? He could have stopped a long time ago, and enjoyed virtually the same level of comfort with a lot less headache. But he loved the headache. He loved the rush and he loved winning. But winning against what, or whom?

Birthdays, ever since he turned fifty, perhaps further back, made him think of death. Shahbaz did not like thinking about death; it was a country with too little confirmed data. But death was indefatigable in its patience and popped into his mind in the most unsuspecting of moments: in the middle of a meeting on land appraisals, while supervising his garden on an uncommonly free afternoon, or toasting an awards dinner. It definitely knew to ambush his birthdays.

One had to get busy; it was the only way to keep death's debilitating shadow out of one's mind. Far to the east, he could see Khondoker's new tower rising. The cheapskate had snuck into Badda for this project; a steel skeleton hovered at Shahbaz Tower's shoulder height. Shahbaz could just see Khondoker, his large frame stooped over his plans. Did he really think that he could somehow thrust up a teetering pole on cheaper land to rival Shahbaz's supremacy? Other side of the lake didn't count, you asshole! Sadly, in this land of illiterates, the wretch had every chance of securing a place in what passed for the public mind.

Khondoker, once his main man and fired just a few years back for uncontrolled thievery, took it up as a mission to upstage his former boss.

The upstart managed to round up a bevy of investors right away and openly tried to poach Shahbaz's plots and clients. When Shahbaz built the tallest tower, he knew Khondoker would come after that too. But this bit of insolence, Shahbaz had prepared for. He had laid a foundation for ten additional floors, and kept the provision secret even from most of his own staff. Finish your gambit first, thought Shahbaz, then I'll show you, and the world, who's Master and who's Servant.

"Sir, we have had to make a small change in the menu," said Neela.

Shahbaz knitted his brows tightly into a joint. Anyone else would read that as a sign of impending thunder, but Neela, his assistant, was amazingly unafraid of him.

"The Indonesian crabs flown in from Singapore went bad," she said. "The caterer had a faulty ice-machine. But, I've found someone who can deliver fresh-caught lobsters from Kuakata for tonight."

He spared a nod of assent and turned back to the window. This was why Neela never got yelled at. She was the only one who came to him with solutions. All the other monkeys came with problems. Or they were the source of problems. Neela was calmness incarnate. She hardly ever smiled, eschewed chitchat. Draped always in dark, subdued saris, hair pinned into a tight bun, she managed to be attractive and forbidding at the same time. How did a girl so young possess so much composure? She came from quite an ordinary family; the father was an engineer in some ministry until paralyzed by an early stroke. Unlike his children, she had the benefit of no fancy schooling, and she'd never been abroad until joining his company. Yet she could run this company someday.

But his own children?

Belkis hated it when Shahbaz compared their kids to anyone, especially any employees. But he had to recognize the facts with pained clarity, even if he was not allowed to utter them. What went wrong? Was he too hard with them? Was Belkis too permissive? Imtiaz and Sonya could not run a stall at a charity fair if they tried! Maybe it was one of nature's wicked acts of wit: letting a recessive gene of softness from his sweet, well-meaning father–a lover of Gibbon, teacher of children, general neighborhood do-gooder–bypass him completely to bloom ferociously in his progeny.

Shahbaz took a few phone calls in between updates on the RSVPs for the night. An irate client needed to be assuaged at his level; the woman was a close relative of the leader of the opposition. You never knew what these people might perceive as a slight. There were calls, too, from his lawyer and from the Commissioner of Police. Then came the drawings for a conclave of luxury residences–a new concept for Dhaka, at least on this scale–and the architects, with their habitual convolutions, ate into the time for the next meeting.

Every phone call, every meeting, could potentially bring news of a calamity. They certainly caused annoyance. But Shahbaz did not mind; in fact, he loved the incessant busyness. It kept him from thinking about death or his family.

Neela came in again. "Sir, there was the interview."

An interview, today? It was not the kind of day when he'd schedule an interview.

"This was the man referred by the Minister."

Ah, that one! Shahbaz had tried to dodge this as long as he could, but the Minister, like all true bumpkins, was impervious to hints. As the largest developer in the country, and with investments in almost a dozen other sectors, there was virtually not a ministry that his company didn't have to deal with. He could not afford to piss any one of them off. Still, the constant nibbling for favors irritated him. He seemed to mind that more than he minded the bribes because the favors were not even counted as favors but taken as his dues to society. Baboons sent him other baboons for discounts on this or that property. The minute a baboon made minister it stopped paying rent. And the worst, when a big baboon sent him a baby baboon to hire for his company.

"May I come in, sir?"

Ah, the baboon was not entirely without training! Shahbaz, who was by now seated back at his enormous black desk, turned towards the door. Neela stood just two steps behind the boy, not ahead, to see if the candidate knew how to make an entrance. She never failed even the smallest details.

The boy was not much older than his son. But something in his expression suggested an intimacy with grimness. Shahbaz gestured for the candidate to take a seat. He was turned out properly enough in a white shirt and black pants. But the face gave Shahbaz a pause. Physically it was like the thousands he saw on the street every day: faces molded out of the very earth of this country–muddy, brown silt and with a hint of incompleteness in the features. But, something about this candidate's visage caught Shahbaz's attention. Shahbaz prided himself on his ability to read people. In a tiny tic, one ill-chosen word, the slobs and the feckless gave themselves away. But every now and then chance presented him an enigma.

"So, you know the Minister?" Shahbaz asked, trying to conceal his malice behind a smile.

"Yes, sir, he is from our village," said the boy.

"Nice for all you villagers that ministers now hail from villages! Once they used to come from cities."

"Yes sir, most people in this country are from the village," said the boy, not quite backing down.

"But should people who need to run a state be from villages? Shouldn't they have a greater exposure of the world?"

"Yes sir, that would be helpful," said the boy.

Helpful, not necessary! There it was again! A certain spikiness. He felt it the moment the chap entered his room. It was there in the stiffness of his body, the impassivity of his face, now in his diction. He had opinions, and he did not surrender them easily. Not the typical supplicant. In theory, Shahbaz knew he should like them, people of independent opinions, but in reality they annoyed him to no end.

"Why did you ask the Minister for a referral?" Shahbaz asked.

"There was no other way to meet a person like you, sir," said the boy.

"Why did you have to meet me? Why not just apply like everyone else?"

"I did, sir," said the boy. "But I was not selected then."

"So, failing to qualify, you tried a connection?"

"No sir, that was not what I meant. The boy who got selected, he got a second class. He can barely speak English. I have a first class. I am better in every way."

"Then why were you not selected?"

"Connections are active at every level, sir," said the boy, undaunted.

This was not the first time Shahbaz had heard of such a charge. He knew the country was full of fucking thieves and cheats. He fought them daily, inside and outside. They proliferated like locusts. Khondoker was the worst he had ever seen. By the end, he had practically formed a gang of his own inside the company. He was trying effectively to hold Shahbaz hostage with everything he knew—and could reveal—and by making himself and his loyals indispensable in various ways. Shahbaz cleaned out the whole lot of them with Khondoker, but he knew that new cliques were forming again in remote corners. All this Shahbaz knew, but this was the first time he heard it from an interviewee. No perspiration on his forehead, no fidgeting in the chair.

"Why blame others when you are using a connection yourself?"

"They did it to commit a wrong, sir. I am trying to rectify it," said the boy with no hint of fear, nor arrogance, but as a mere presentation of fact.

Shahbaz rolled his chair a few inches back from the desk, as if to afford a broader perspective of the exhibit before him. Something about the boy reminded Shahbaz of his young self. He too was bold enough to walk into places where he did not belong and make demands to which he had no title.

Where did it come from, that daring? Certainly not his father. He was a meek man. By the standards of his peasant stock, his father had risen far. A teacher in the local school, which back then boasted an

English principal. Mr. Stuart was a fearsome and lore-filled figure of Shahbaz's childhood. The man's simplest habits—the sparseness of his diet, his long walks, his ability to surprise students and staff with quiet appearances during their leisure—were regarded as matters of unique virtue, emblematic of a superior race. Shahbaz could vividly recall Stuart in a short-sleeved green shirt, the chest-pocket stained with the pens he clipped to it, sitting at his desk, peering venomously at his visitors over his round glasses. A few wisps of hair, aided by a languid, long-stemmed ceiling fan, wiped his flaky pate.

In Shahbaz's weltanschauung, Stuart represented the worst kind of pervert. He abjured pleasures which he had no ability to access in the first place. But he used these false sacrifices to justify the right to reproach others. Stuart made rounds of the neighborhood tut-tutting grown men for flicking cigarette butts on the road or dumping trash outside their houses, chiding boys for shooting out street lights with their homemade slings, and robbing young girls all the joys of their nubility with his withering asexual glance.

In emulation of Mr. Stuart, Shahbaz's father, too, dressed simply, in flowing white kurtas and ate only twice a day, that too the diet of a monk in severe penitence. Being fundamentally a good man, however, he lacked Stuart's low cunning and failed to turn his abnegations into a sadistic leverage over others. Yet religiously he related every habit and action of Mr. Stuart at their funereal family dinners. Most painfully, Shahbaz recalled how his father would jot down in his diligent little diary the utterances of Mr. Stuart, which were nothing but platitudes and homilies, plucked no doubt from some *vade mecum* of colonial conduct.

Shahbaz despised the Stuarts of the world. He hated the Baboons and the Khondokers just as much. The Softies alone—like his father, his wife, and his children—he did not hate, though they sure made it hard for him to love them at times. How he came to be related to so many Softies on all sides was one of nature's great mysteries. Still, the Softies had their beauty and charm and were far superior to the other types. The others he regarded outright as enemies. Long before he attained the vocabulary to give any definite form to these thoughts, they existed as feelings and found a kinetic expression in his reflexes.

One day Stuart ordered the morning assembly to kneel down to atone for some authorless vandalism of school property, but Shahbaz alone refused to bend. To this day, Shahbaz could see that moment vividly: tattered white clouds sculled across a pristine blue sky, and a gentle spring breeze heaved the national flag to slow and interrupted swells. Rows and columns of dark bowed heads extended before him, behind him and to both sides. Stuart and his twelve-year-old self faced off. Shahbaz needed only to close his eyes to see Stuart's gray face elongated in complete disbelief at an urchin's defiance to his unchallenged rule.

Shahbaz stood transfixed by the velocity of his own power. Not even expulsion from school, nor his father's agonized sermons diminished the delectable, palpable sensation that was revealed to him in that early accident. He knew that no one could take that ballista of power away from him. It came from within and for the simple reason that he did not fear the consequences that paralyzed others.

When his father secured him an admission at the best college in their division, he chose to head for the capital with no admission, not much money, nor any notable contacts. Counseled, again by his father, to take a government job, he entered the private sector. Right after independence, due for a promotion, he decided to quit the firm, again to his father's shock, and started trading and contracting on his own. What a furious fortune he made right away on Russian wheat, Turkish spices, and edible oil from Brazil and Malaysia! And repairs of war-devastated roads and bridges. By picking up enemy properties and turning around abandoned mills. He missed the incredible rush of those days; he pushed all paper and planning work to the night hours to avoid losing a single minute during the day for meetings.

Shahbaz's poor father watched his exploits with disapproving dismay from a distance. There is no peace, no peace my son, in this kind of living, he told him when Shahbaz cajoled him into coming to the capital on holidays. The poor man died disappointed that, while a teacher to the world, he was unable to educate his own son. It was true Shahbaz took little from his father. But it wasn't the case that he didn't take anything at all. He got his taste in reading–historical novels–from his father, and so many years later, they were his principal pastime and solace. Never mind that his father and he drew utterly different, even opposing, lessons from the same tale. The man never quite understood the moves Shahbaz made, neither the jubilant gains nor the inevitable failures and certainly not the first act of defiance that set him free.

Even after a thousand recalls, the moment felt as joltingly fresh as an unsuspecting burst of liquorice in one's mouth. Shahbaz relished the memory for an extra second and then unlidded his eyes to appraise again the candidate sent by the Minister.

What species of deviation was this rooted before him? Neither a Softie, nor a Khondoker. Neither a Baboon pure nor exactly a Stuart. Yet elements of all the categories seemed to jostle for primacy in its bosom. Shahbaz hated Hybrids! They were hard to read and harder still to manage. You never knew how or when they'd act up. Much better a toiler, not too dull, who followed instructions. A toiler he could have easily stashed away in his vast marketing juggernaut. But what to do with this porcupine? After another moment of deliberation–given that this was his birthday and this the Minister's man–he chose to be charitable.

"Look, son, you seem well-meaning. So let me give you a piece of advice. Don't judge the world so much. The world is what it is. And you have to make a way in it somehow."

"I understand, sir, but in this case, I really felt I deserved that position."

"Why are you so fixated on that position? Or this company? With your connection, why not just try somewhere else?"

The boy leaned forward, catching the table's edge with his fingertips, like a mountaineer desperate for anchor. But before he could speak, Neela peered in. Eye-to-eye Shahbaz secured the information that the matter was important. Line 1 was beeping. It had to be taken.

"Hello?"

"Hello, Baba, did you forget we were having lunch today?"

Shit! It was Imtiaz. This was what happened when he made his own appointments—and then also forgot to update Neela.

"Forget? No, Imtiaz, why would I forget? I'm just running really late."

The night before Imtiaz had come into his study, a large room of leather furniture and soft, deep rugs, where Shahbaz sat ensconced in a silk robe, feet on the ottoman. This was where he revived himself, all alone, at the end of his long days. Unless he had any pressing business reports or backlog of correspondence, this was a time to open a bottle of liqueur and a good historical novel. At the moment, he was immersed in a magnificent fantasy about Ubar, a lost city of the Arabs.

Imtiaz punctured that delicious reprieve to invite him to lunch at Sublime.

"A birthday treat?" Shahbaz had asked hopefully.

Imtiaz shrugged, but said nothing. He was such a stiff fellow; how could two charismatic parents spawn such an awkward child? Luck truly had a wicked sense of humor and balanced every excess of blessing in one department of life with a smiting in other areas. Still, Shahbaz was touched that the boy asked at all. Logistically, it was not the best day for them to have lunch, but as he stared at Imtiaz—gangly and sullen, shoulder hunched, fingers jutting into the pockets of his stylishly frayed jeans—a warm fatherly feeling purled in some long-unvisited compartment of his many-compartmented heart.

This sensation of warmth, superior to the one induced by his nightly cordials, was not available to him nearly as often as it once was. Back then his children were still children. Saturday mornings were spent in the Club, playing water polo with the kids. More splashing and screaming than sport, but what fun they had those days. Belkis, full of laughter, didn't suffer from headaches.

"Sure, I'd love to have lunch tomorrow," said Shahbaz. He wanted to ask Imtiaz to sit down, to share a swig of Benedictine. But the boy was out the door as quickly and quietly as he had entered, leaving Shahbaz with his private thoughts. Imtiaz would not simply treat him to lunch for his birthday. May be there was something more to it. Did the boy change his mind after all? Maybe he wanted to join Shahbaz's company? It was sweet of him to choose Shahbaz's birthday to present such news. Shahbaz could not imagine a better gift.

How could he forget this lunch, of all things?

"I'll be there in no time. Are you at the restaurant already?"

"Yes, I've been here at least twenty minutes," said Imtiaz, unable to hide a hint of irritation.

Shahbaz looked at his watch. The mid-day traffic would be an absolute killer. He was in no mood, given the nature of the day, to spend so much time on the road, but he did not want to test his strained relations with Imtiaz further with a last-minute cancellation. Besides, against all odds, a part of him was curious, even hopeful, to see if Imtiaz might not surprise him on his birthday.

Later that day, indeed even months later when the Minister turned hostile, Shahbaz wondered if that morning, and especially that interview, might have gone differently if he had not been interrupted by Imtiaz's call at that precise juncture. The phone call threw him off his balance. He felt irritated with himself for forgetting the lunch. And with Imtiaz for being the way he was. Why could Imtiaz not be like ten other sons in the city and just join his firm? Or organize his birthday party instead of taking him out to lunch?

And there was always some claimant for his precious time, like the cadet of rectitude still planted before him. How much more courtesy could the Minister wish for? He had met the Minister's man. He would put him in the files, but with a high priority marking.

"Listen, I wish I could talk to you more, but as you see I'm running late," said Shahbaz.

Neela hovered at the door to see off the guest, and to take any last minute instructions before Shahbaz headed out.

"Sir, before I leave, if I may..."

"Yes, what is it?" Shahbaz asked, impatient.

"Sir, you asked why I wanted this job. It's because I really wanted to get something on my own merit."

The thread of their conversation had in fact evaporated in Shahbaz's mind. But, when the boy mentioned it, the point of interruption came back to him, and with it came a sudden quickening of breath, a tightening of the neck muscles.

"I did not ask why you wanted this job, but why you wanted to work for my company. Why try so hard here?"

"Because I really did qualify for that position, sir, but it was taken away from me."

"So, it's all about you?" Shahbaz said sharply, voice rising, as he left his chair. "You don't give a damn about us, it's all just about you!"

"That's not how I meant it, sir," stammered the boy. In his attempt to rise quickly, he knocked his chair over, and its steel frame clanged loudly against the marble floor. Neela was now one step outside the office, gesturing to someone with silent urgency.

The conversation-long indeterminacy about the cad suddenly came to an end. They were not similar in any aspect–that was clear. Shahbaz never went in anywhere to plead for justice, to flaunt his righteousness, and he certainly had sense enough not to say things that might offend the person from whom he expected a favor. But this boy committed all those offenses–the boy was no Shahbaz, he was a fucking Stuart. A local variant, perhaps a sub-species, but he was a constipated, self-righteous humbug.

"I entertained you this long just out of courtesy to the Minister," said Shahbaz, as a sudden spasm of anger gripped his scalp like an electric cap. "You think the world owes you something 'cause you pissed well on some exam paper? You think that's how the world works you ignorant self-righteous fool?"

Don't hit him! Don't hit him! A voice from some unclouded part of his cerebrum counseled Shahbaz, even as he strode away from his desk. The boy was trying to lift the chair back up without taking his eyes off of Shahbaz. "Get out, get out of my office," shouted Shahbaz as he approached the boy. The boy dropped the chair with another metal jangle.

Shahbaz was now two feet away from the offender. The boy, drained of all courage or entitlement, stood with both palms raised, half in apology and half in defense.

"The world owes you nothing," thundered Shahbaz, jabbing a finger at his terrorized prey. "The world owes no one anything, you understand?"

The boy was sweating profusely by now, and kept trying to revise his meaning, but every attempt at a new sentence, in his fear and confusion, strewn with "Sir's" and "Sorry's," ended as an unfinished exordium.

Shahbaz took one more step forward, and the boy, attempting to step back caught the back of his ankle and tripped. He arrested the momentum with both hands, but came to rest only in a tangle with the fallen chair. From nowhere a security guard rushed over to help. Shahbaz watched the spectacle with a look of pure disgust and then turned abruptly to find Neela just inside the door. "Where do you find these people?" Shahbaz shouted at Neela, as he marched towards the door. "Why do you let them come to me? Is this what I pay you for?"

Neela stood quietly, holding out his blazer. Even as he abused her, Shahbaz knew it was not her fault. At least he did not strike the misfit. That would have been hard to justify to the Minister. He had vowed that morning not to lose his temper on his birthday. Not to shout at anyone. But the provocations never ceased. You had to protect yourself, thought Shahbaz, as he descended to the parking lot in a scented, carpeted private elevator. Eat or be eaten. That was the law, and he allowed no one, big or small, to get even a nibble of his flesh.

The Minister would not like it. No, the man won't like it much at all, said Shahbaz to himself, settling into the cabin of his extra-long black Mercedes. But the Minister, too, could afford to be only so piqued at his biggest patron over a trifle. Too bad it had to happen on his birthday and right before lunch with Imtiaz. He would have liked to be in a better mood to meet his son. Luckily, he found the inside of his car almost as recuperative as his study. It muffled all noise down to a hush, thanks to its heavy bulletproof encasing. He would see the Minister at his party that night. And as long as he got to tell his story first, things should be fine, he told himself as the car progressed haltingly through traffic to his destination.

From the moment Shahbaz disembarked from his car, he was ushered, through all the transit points—entrance, reception, lift, restaurant—by a retinue of unnecessarily senior staff, like a parcel in a children's game. A gigantic red Chinese lamp hung from the ceiling of the small restaurant, augmenting the intimate feeling, amazingly, without detracting one iota from its classiness.

Imtiaz was easy to spot, even when seated. Spiky hair added a superfluous inch to his figure. As if all this weren't enough, the boy wore a white T-shirt, a pair of large pink lips painted suggestively on his chest.

"Hi, Baba," the boy said as he uncorked slowly to his full height.

Shahbaz extended his hand for a shake, but the boy pulled him in closer for a full embrace. He was indifferent to the crew of waiters surrounding them as he completed his sign of affection. At least he left Shahbaz the corner seat; it was nice of him to remember that Shahbaz did not like to sit with a room to his back.

"I'm so sorry, Imtiaz," said Shahbaz, as he settled into a chair pulled back and slid forward with perfect timing by a waiter. This perch afforded him a view of the entire room, and he scanned the place to ensure that there was no one in the vicinity that he would want to avoid. He didn't know how other people collected so many friends. He suspected friendships were a function of lives led in frivolity or in innocuous and inoffensive submission.

A waiter handed them menus and another brought around cold towels—a nice new touch. "It's been such a crazy day already, you won't believe it."

"Even on your birthday, Baba?" said Imtiaz. "You should have taken the day off. It's your sixtieth, for god's sake."

"Oh, don't think I don't try," Shahbaz said. "But you won't believe the things that happen in my day, the shits that show up in my office."

"And this is what you want me to join?" Imtiaz said, with a chuckle to soften the unexpected gibe.

Shahbaz chose to ignore the comment, though it was not too propitious for his hopes.

"Shall we order first?" asked Shahbaz in an effort to stay neutral.

"I had two rounds of appetizers while waiting for you, Baba," said Imtiaz. "You go right ahead. I'm going to have dessert."

"Well, you can't just sit there while I chomp on my food," said Shahbaz, trying to rescue a symmetry in their positions.

"Fine, order me a salad then," said Imtiaz.

Shahbaz only had to look up for a waiter to appear with a pen and order pad.

"A seafood marinara for me," he ordered. "A soup for the boy. Two glasses of wine. No, make it a bottle!"

"It's on the house, sir, in honor of your birthday," reported the smiling waiter in response.

Shahbaz looked at Imtiaz, who arched his brows to say, I didn't even tell them! "Fine," said Shahbaz, closing the menu, "but no cakes and no singing."

He liked to order quickly, and he also liked attention but hated any fuss.

From where they sat they could see cars speeding away on Airport Road. Traffic seemed light for the hour. And in the distance, a plane making a slow arc down towards the airport.

Shahbaz tried to regale Imtiaz with the story of the strange candidate. But Imtiaz didn't seem to fully appreciate the absurdity of the situation. I hope the boy wasn't hurt, he said. Having no gift for small talk and after this thwarted effort at lightness, Shahbaz decided to be direct, "So, Imtiaz, did you have anything in mind, or is this just a birthday lunch for your old man?"

"Actually, there is something," said Imtiaz, evidently relieved that he didn't have to find a segue to the topic.

By now Shahbaz could tell that there was no great surprise, at least none that could count as a birthday gift for him. Yet some part of him that struggled to stay human could not help but cling to the rare notes of optimism involving his family.

"I know this is not the best day to tell you this," said Imtiaz. "But there is a deadline tomorrow."

Ah, the hopes of his liqueur-soaked nocturnes, they never could withstand daylight! That much he knew, yet he felt deflated.

"You see Baba, UCLA offered me a scholarship. Actually it's from a Foundation, but for UCLA. Normally, they are reserved for Americans, but they made an exception for me. That's how much they like my stuff. I must send in my acceptance tomorrow."

Shahbaz had heard the boy speak of film school in passing, but he had never paid attention to any timeline involving the scheme. A waiter placed a steaming dish of seafood marinara in front of Shahbaz. His son was garrulous with praise of his chosen school, and the rare honors they had bestowed on him. The boy was completely indifferent to the food. Each morsel shifted down Shahbaz's gullet like moistened Styrofoam balls, without registering any flavor on his palate.

"Baba, aren't you going to say something?" asked Imtiaz finally.

"What's there to say? You are leaving me," said Shahbaz.

"Is that all you can think of? Aren't you even a little bit proud of me?"

"Of course, I am proud of you," said Shahbaz, never suspending his lunch. "I've always been proud of you. But, you could have worked with me for a couple of years before going away."

"We've been through this, Baba," said Imtiaz. "You know once I get into the business, I'll never get out. Not for film. It's now or never."

Shahbaz looked up, pushing away his half-finished plate. You are such a boy, Imtiaz! You're still such a boy! Film is just another diversion for you. What was he now, twenty-three, twenty-four? At that age, Shahabaz thought...oh hell, what was the point?

"I'm proud of you, Imtiaz," said Shahbaz as he looked at the boy's imploring face.

Shahbaz had left his own father behind by a couple of generations. What he knew to wear or say, how he knew to look at the world and the things in it, in all this he was separated from his father by not less than two generations. Imtiaz should have been the one to consolidate all his gains, but as if in another generational leap, the boy was rushing them to dissipation.

"What kind of films will you make, Imtiaz?" asked Shahbaz as the boy's elaborate chocolate dessert finally arrived. The question prompted another dam-breaking torrent on world cinema, on fresh angles and new takes, on influences. Between mouthfuls of chocolate the boy rattled off names like Wong-Kar Wai and Takeshi Kitano. Also, the Coen Brothers and the Wachowski Brothers.

Shahbaz remembered how furniture stores in Dhaka, before they became a diversion for rich men's wives, and took on boutique forms with artistic names, were always known by the name of Such-and-Such Brothers Ltd. Odd that world-famous filmmakers today should enjoy appellations of the same format, he thought. Before Shahbaz could share this little joke with Imtiaz though, the boy left his chair abruptly. He had to collect prints to send to some short film festival—there was a deadline for that too.

Shahbaz paid the bill for the lunch and debated going back to the office. Once inside his car though, he decided on home. Even the iron-clad vessel that was his heart could sustain only so many squalls on a single day.

Shahbaz's car proceeded through the immobilized roads of Dhaka with all the tricks known to local drivers: juts and jags to fill up any bubble of navigable space that opened up, lane-cutting and lane-straddling, bivouacking through supposed shortcuts, light-bumping non-motorized vehicles, threatening to run over peddlers and pedestrians with a set of tires rolled onto pavements, turning without signals into one-way streets, running red lights, and ignoring the sign language of ill-paid traffic cops with the same disdain with which pigeons feel free to shit on the world. And all the while one tried to drown out the protests of all competitors with the dumb, brutish, incessant bleating of their electric horns.

Shahbaz felt sad from his lunch with Imtiaz. He could not say he was terribly surprised, still anticipation didn't make bad news more palatable.

Shahbaz wondered what would become of his company after him. He knew it would disintegrate but in what manner exactly? Would it shrink to a much smaller size under a less generative but tidy management? Couldn't Sonya handle even that much?

Shahbaz had inducted Sonya, despite some initial hesitation on her part, into the interior decoration division of his company. He started the unit itself two years ago precisely for the purpose of enticing the girl into the business. Perhaps she'd find it more appealing than other facets of the business and one needed to enter somewhere.

He had noticed, not without a whit of mirth, that the wife or daughter of every rich man in town fancied herself to be a designer of clothes, spaces, or furniture. They opened up boutiques of strange, flowing, hybrid garments; shops for bags and jewelry studded with large and uncommon stones; outlets for shoes spangled with metal gewgaws or fabric swatches. To say nothing of the posh galleries for bad art. If these vendors of redundancy could have a game in town, why not Sonya?

She was smarter than most of her peers, and he persuaded her to take a few short courses in New York and Singapore. Don't worry about men, he told her. You need to focus on work for a change. Husband, kids, all that will happen in due course. Thirty was not an age to worry about, he assured her in all sincerity. Not with the kind of money I'm going to leave you—that part of the thought he kept to himself.

As the car pulled into his driveway, Shahbaz noticed a troop of workers sitting in the middle of a lawn, surrounded by clusters of un-assembled materials. Shahbaz owned one of the older and over-sized

Gulshan plots. A tall siris tree stood sentry at the northern perimeter, and in its shade a majestic white colonnaded house took up almost half the property. Back when such shenanigans were possible, Shahbaz stitched the neighboring plot to his own to expand the lawn, which rolled to the streetside in a gentle, man-made undulation.

He planned to have the entire green covered with a beautiful silky blue canopy and chairs and tables with matching drapery, even orchids of the same color to adorn each table. A bandstand in the corner. Three serving stations and set apart from them, a bar. They could open up the entire ground floor if it started to drizzle or if all five hundred invitees actually showed up.

As he paused for an inspection though, signs of things falling behind schedule began to emerge. The metal frame for the lawn-sized canopy was piled up in one corner and no supervisor in sight. The workers seemed as if they were paid to wait around. One of them sat on small pile of folded chairs, slightly apart from the main group, dangling a crossed leg and about to flick a bidi onto the lawn itself.

Shahbaz trampled through the strip of flowerbed lining the lawn straight toward the culprit to catch him in flagrant dereliction.

Noticing Shahbaz's combative march, the other workers fled to different corners of the lawn and picked up disparate items of equipment. One fellow started hammering a tent peg into a random spot in the lawn. Another began to unspool a melon-sized ball of twine to no evident purpose. Through this sudden flurry of activity they kept an eye on Shahbaz while the hapless leg-dangler was still blissfully unaware of either Shahbaz's approach or the frenzied dispersal of his colleagues. He was busy counting how many bidis were left in his packet—one had to space them out properly and not run out too soon into a shift.

Shahbaz came right up to the man, who now was about to turn, perhaps sensing a flux in the air-volume in his environment. But it was too late. Before the man could straighten up even to an early hominid stature, Shahbaz grabbed him by the collar and yanked him with his full might. Shahbaz was not exceedingly tall like his son, nor did he boast the strength of his vigorous youth. But he misjudged his strength when he was angry, and though he meant only to tug the man to a standing position, he sent him tumbling into the ground.

"What is this? What is this? What the fuck is wrong with you people? The party starts in three hours and nothing is up yet! You haven't done a thing!"

Shahbaz was livid with rage, and the listless faces of the workers deepened his frustration. They didn't know who he was. What the event was about. They were paid to put things up, move them around, carry them, take them down. They didn't know or care what was supposed to start when. They were told to come here, and they were going about at their normal pace of business.

How did he ever get anything done here? How did anyone? Shahbaz felt almost on the verge of tears. What was wrong with his people? What was it? Too much fucking silt in the blood? Opium in the breast milk? Cavities in the reasoning parts of the brain? What was it?

By now, Belkis had appeared at the verandah overlooking the lawn. And servants rushed out onto the driveway. Shahbaz was on the phone with Neela.

"Neela, what is going on here? Have you seen this place? Who are these guys? Whom have you sent?"

"It's all under control, sir," came Neela's calming voice from the other end. "I'm in touch with the decorators, they sent the wrong crew. Don't worry everything will be ready by seven."

Shahbaz usually took longer to climb down from one of his angry peaks, but there was Belkis in the verandah, staring at him with a look balanced perfectly between a reproach and an appeal.

"Come inside, Shahbaz," said Belkis. "Don't be so angry on your birthday."

"Do you see what they're doing? It's going to be a disaster tonight. The crabs didn't come. And now these monkeys fucking around when they should be putting things up."

"You don't need to worry about that. It will all work out," said Belkis with an uncanny air of certitude.

Shahbaz vacillated for a moment between his natural instinct to pursue the matter further, and a need to succumb to the accumulations of the day, to which he had by now added three glasses of wine. Once he reached the verandah, however, Belkis's soft hand on his shoulder tilted him towards a decision to trundle up to his bedroom. Didn't Imtiaz say he should take time off on his birthday? Let the monkeys manage on their own for a change!

Belkis pulled the blackout curtains. The room, like all the spaces he regularly inhabited—his office, his car, his study—was well-insulated from the sounds of his extraordinarily noisy city. Sheltering himself in such a string of cocoons was one of the many tricks with which he kept himself taut for the rounds of light and confrontation. It will work out, Belkis's soothing assurance rang in his ears again, as he lay his head on the pillow, and drifted off to sleep.

Shahbaz loved parties. Not other people's parties, but the ones he engendered. He loved almost every aspect of them. The guest list, the theme. Would there be live music? A band or a soloist? Somebody famous or an unobtrusive professional? With what new ambrosiac rarity on the menu could he awe his guests? He could not abide the casualness with which other people—even his own wife or children—seemed content to plan a party. No, parties—like life itself—were a show, and one had to bring a murderous obsession to every detail, and to their timely execution to ensure a stunning effect.

Shahbaz was not happy about the Indonesian crabs. And he wondered if the orchids had been released by now from customs as he began to dress for the party. He had slept a lot longer than he normally did, if he ever took a nap. But between Imtiaz's news, the wine, and finally the idiot workers, his typical élan was depleted. The sleep would supply him with the reserves needed to glad-hand a few hundred people, to smile on the faces of his enemies.

Shahbaz stood in front of the mirror holding up two shirts, one white and one blue—both fresh from a pricey London store, handmade to his size—against his pale but hairy torso. There was no denying the steady, gradual distension of his gut beneath the skin. He checked himself in silhouette, and despite some resentment against the workings of time, gravity, and his own treacherous body, he decided it was not too bad for sixty. He was far more trim than most of his peers, and for that he should be thankful.

More importantly, the body was still fundamentally healthy. He suffered from high cholesterol, kept under control with medication. And there was a tendency towards hypertension. Also, borderline diabetes. Nothing out of the ordinary for his age or race. Nothing that should lead to a sudden event and land him in a hospital bed, or, his worst fear, confine him to such a bed permanently, hooked to tubes and monitors, with neither the locomotion of life nor the escape of death within reach. Truth be told, as much as he disliked the day-by-day nearing of death, what terrified him was the prospect of unabated, unbearable pain. The indignity of soiling his bedclothes, and having his private parts washed by strangers. No catheters please! If life would grant him that one mercy!

Much rather a premature end, he thought—and could an end be really premature, once you hit sixty?—than the terrible debility of a terminal disease.

Shahbaz chose the blue shirt, clasping the double French cuffs with a pair of gold links. The process of getting dressed for a party was usually sufficient to put him into a good mood. But neither the siesta, nor the ritual of donning a brand new vestment, in which he could often find a childish pleasure, managed to dispel the sense of imbalance with which he had come to bed. Shahbaz completed his attire with a simple black suit, and headed downstairs to check on the setup.

When he came down to the drawing room, though, he found Belkis and Sonya seated with a tray of tea in front of them. Imtiaz, a little apart, fiddled with a camera. The picture of his beautiful wife, and handsome children, all together and dressed for his party, elevated his mood for a moment.

"You're up already," said Belkis. "I was just about to come up and wake you."

"I am ready, as you see, as ready as I'll ever be to turn sixty," said Shahbaz, holding out his hands, and then coming up to their little circle in the front part of the drawing room.

Through the sheers on the French doors, he could see the canopy now fully erected. Tables, draped in silky blue cloth, supported quivering lamp-lights—and yes, blue Thai orchids. Shahbaz walked up to the French doors, parted the sheers to gain a better look. A team of waiters, dressed smartly in white shirts and black pants, wended through the rows, laying down plates. Neela was talking to the band in a corner.

Belkis had suggested a flautist. Neela a classical singer. But Shahbaz selected a young band to play covers of songs from their youth.

Things seemed to be in order. He walked back to the family. Belkis held out a cup of tea toward him.

"You look lovely," he said, taking the cup from her. The compliment was entirely sincere. As he knew to expect, she did look stunning, in a stylish black chiffon sari, while diamonds sparkled subtly, not just from her necklace or earrings, but also from her hairpin and watchband. With her it was never the clothes or ornaments, though; it was a light within herself that, despite all her indeterminate afflictions, she could still switch on at will.

"You look mighty spiffy yourself, Baba," said Sonya. She didn't quite inherit her mother's looks, but could be arresting in her own way, as she was in a maroon sari.

"Yes, we're a marvelous looking set. We should take photos," said Imtiaz, getting up to mount the camera on a stand he'd already set up.

The boy was made easily uncomfortable by these moments, when they were together, dressed up, and supposed to feel like a family, or have special feelings in that capacity.

"There will be plenty of time for pictures," said Shahbaz. "Let's just enjoy the tea. Meantime, maybe Imtiaz can go change?"

Belkis cast a look at Shahbaz as if to say, Not now, please, don't spoil this moment.

"Change? You don't like this?" Imtiaz said, pulling at his long-sleeve white T-shirt. "It's been hand-painted by Shahabuddin. He did it for a charity."

"It's wonderful, and I'm sure the cause was worthy. It just doesn't fit in with the mood of the party."

"Baba, I got you one of these for your birthday," said Imtiaz, in mock vexation, not taking the father's challenge too seriously. "Shahabuddin bhai was so nice about it, he did your portrait!"

"With half my face missing? Isn't that his style? It's a nice thought, Imtiaz; thanks. But, go, please, put on a proper shirt for tonight, can't you?"

Imtiaz dropped his smile. Then chucked the lens cap at a sofa. He walked away without another word.

Belkis looked askance at Shahbaz. Really, was that necessary? She was right. What difference did it make how the boy dressed? The world knew he was a misfit. At least he was not a drug addict. Children of half his friends seemed to be perpetually in and out of rehab.

Sonya put her cup down. "Really, Baba, why are you so hard on Imtiaz?"

"He's not dressed right for the evening. And I can't even say that?"

"It's your birthday, Shahbaz. Be nice to everyone," said Belkis.

"Everyone should be nice to me," said Shahbaz with a laugh. "He's running off again, and waits till my birthday to give the news."

"He only heard of the scholarship a week ago," said Sonya, coming again to her brother's defense.

"So he could find time to tell you, and you," said Shahbaz, looking by turns at Belkis and Sonya. "But me—"

Shahbaz needed to vent the frustrations he had swallowed quietly at lunch. But before he could complete his thoughts, Neela peeked into the room.

"What, what is it now?" Shahbaz asked.

Neela walked up to where the three of them sat, evidently all three annoyed to be interrupted.

"Sir, the singer's thrown his back out. He can't even stand up."

"Let them just play the songs," said Sonya. "No need for the singing."

Shahbaz looked at Sonya, and then again to Neela to see if she could offer any other solutions. "The keyboard player says he knows most of the songs. Would you like to hear him a little?"

"No, never mind. Either the guy turns up, or like Sonya said, it'll be instrumentals only."

Neela nodded, and went out again. Belkis got up to go find Imtiaz. Sonya wanted to go finish her makeup. They put down their teas. Always an interruption, always a surprise. The guests would start arriving any moment; this was no time to start a rehearsal. Shahbaz sat alone, and slowly sipped at his tea, and fortified himself for the invited hordes.

When Shahbaz stepped out to the verandah, the sky was just dark enough to bring out the effects of the lighting. The extra altitude of the canopy worked just as he knew it would. Bloody crabs, bloody singer, all these details aside, things looked good. The guests would never know what other effects were meant for them, any more than his clients knew what amazing tiles he was actually going to put into their bathrooms.

Shahbaz loved this moment, right before the arrival of the guests. Wondering who would actually turn up, and in what sequence. He loved how the people dressed up—for that effort alone he could momentarily forgive them. That they took the trouble to dress up, to show up, to smile, and, in the case of some of the characters, who knew how, to make an event out of the entrance itself, dismembering the greeting into an unexpected blitz of queries, quips and compliments, and then binding it back into coherence with a tourniquet of wit—ah, that was what he waited for, that was the gift!

But first came the relatives, a moribund and dutiful bunch, who obviated any hopes for brilliance. They intoned the customary benisons—"long life," "good health," "greater fortunes"—but an irritated Shahbaz registered the real thoughts lurking behind their brows: a nephew who hoped to enlist as a supplier for his shoddy products; a white-haired aunt, an imbecile, who day-dreamed about Imtiaz falling for one of her chubby daughters.

This sudden spit of venom took Shahbaz himself by surprise. No, he didn't feel all right. By now, typically a party ought to have put him in a much better mood, but it was as if the world had skipped a revolution this morning, and now nothing could get back into rhythm.

Shahbaz stood near the gate itself, personally welcoming every guest, even as he cursed some of them silently in his mind. Belkis and Sonya took turns by his side, but Imtiaz wandered at a distance, talking to the band. When will you grow up, my boy? How many more years?

At least the bugger's a got a proper shirt on now, thought Shahbaz, as he greeted a couple of ministers, and a few broad-grinning MP's. All of them had asked him for money before the election and whenever the mood struck—yet delivered little or fitfully when he needed a favor. Smile, smile all you want now, you baboons; party's in power, now's the time for you to strut and present your flowering rumps to the world and to raid and take over all you can. Don't worry, the fun won't last.

The arrival of an old school friend, the only one he was still in touch with, stanched this bilious upsurge for a moment. Then it resumed with the appearance of a newspaper editor, a first-rate, mongoose-faced Stuart. Lawyers of the Supreme Court, a slew of bankers, and various stripes of hypocrites, in an unceasing procession. Shahbaz all smiles with every one of them.

There was no sign of the Minister and this bothered him. He had few friends, if any at all, to warm these events; at least, those who ate off his hands should have the decency to swell the crowd. With a glance he beckoned Neela and asked her to check if the man was on his way.

Waiters went around with trays of caviar and sushi. Riesling for those who wanted it and sparkling cider for the innocents. Also, cocktails made out of passion fruit and pomegranates. There was a full bar—they could have whatever they wanted. The guests looked happy and glittery.

Shahbaz could decently abandon the guard post and proceed to mingle with people under the tent. The band started out nicely with a soft Cliff Richard classic. Imtiaz, presumably, had permitted the second man to sing. Shahbaz felt beckoned inside by the music, but just as he was about to turn away, bearing an outlandishly large box, wrapped in an equally outlandish red and gold gift paper, Khondoker arrived.

Ah, the oleaginous pestilence himself! This was the only name on the guest list to which Belkis had raised an objection, not that she liked most of the others either. Why, why would you want to invite him of all people? Shahbaz had his reasons, of course. He did not want to openly snub Khondoker. That he felt would be a greater sign of weakness. Khondoker used to come to all his shindigs when he served under Shahbaz.

Belkis stiffened as the man came up to them, with a huge, yellow, gap-toothed smile. His two sons, dressed like their father in garish punjabis, flanked the man.

"Happy birthday, sir," said Khondoker. "So many happy returns! You look great, sir, you look barely fifty, sir. Can't believe it's your sixtieth already."

Khondoker projected an aura of largeness without being overweight. This was mainly on account of the thickness of his bones. The forehead, widened by a receding hairline, sloped down to thick eyebrows. Jaws, ribcage, knees, every part of him offended anyone with a sense of proportion with their unexpected protuberance.

"It's good of you to come, Khondoker," said Shahbaz, staying coldly neutral inside. Against people of no consequence, he allowed his mind to freely churn up acidic ripostes. But any sighting of a real enemy slowed his pulse down to a level of deep focus.

"How could I miss it, sir? See, I even brought my sons. Salaam, c'mon boys, give salaam to your uncle," said Khondoker, stepping aside to make room for his twins to genuflect and touch Shahbaz's feet.

"There's no need for that, no need for that," protested Shahbaz as the two boys, just a little younger than Imtiaz, dipped down on command to touch his feet.

The boys looked uncannily like their father: broad-framed and bony, but free from the father's lopsidedness or gapped teeth. Merciful corrections from their mother's genes, Shahbaz assumed.

Khondoker passed the large golden parcel to one of the boys and took hold of Shahbaz by the arm. One hand he gripped in a firm shake, and another he placed lightly on the forearm to suggest a deeper bond. Shahbaz hated hand-claspers. It was one of the many things he tried to teach Khondoker when he first came to Shahbaz. But while the ambitious menial picked up on his business tips with voracious rapidity, Shahbaz was able to make little dent on his sartorial sense or social etiquette.

"They're working with me now," said Khondoker. "Such a joy you know, sir, to have your sons in the business. To see the next generation come up."

From the dull obedience in their eyes, Shahbaz could see that the man treated his sons like slaves. Khondoker's shameless and limitless avarice was buttressed now by the support of two able and insensate sons. Jupiter clearly ascendant for Khondoker. Whereas culture, and cultured sensibilities, were his doom.

Khondoker, flanked again by his sons, practically corralled Shahbaz away from the newer arrivals. With a wary eye on Shahbaz, Belkis received the guests who were still trickling in.

"You know, sir, how I respect you. I tell everybody, my boys, that you are my real father. What I know, everything I learned from you."

"Don't say that, Khondoker. You are your own man," said Shahbaz, struggling to be charitable.

"No, sir, I owe it to you, and I never deny it. I say to everyone, what I have today, I owe it all to you," insisted Khondoker.

"I taught many people, Khondoker, but no one else struck out to achieve your kind of success. You must not give me credit that belongs to you," replied Shahbaz. He tried to retrieve his arm with a slight tug, but there was no give from the other side.

"I know you have some hard feelings about me, sir," said Khondoker, taking a step closer and lowering his voice. "But on a day like this, I want to request you to let them go. I don't want you to have any hard feelings about me, sir."

"Let it go Khondoker," said Shahbaz. "There are no hard feelings."

Trust Khondoker to pick a receiving line to start a heart-to-heart. Did the mongrel learn nothing from him at all?

"No, sir, you must say it to me, say it in front of my sons, otherwise I have no peace," said Khondoker.

Say what? Shahbaz was not sure what the man really wanted from him or what this display was really about.

"You are my father, sir, and you are my hero," Khondoker gestured at his boys with a nod of his head, but without taking his hands off of Shahbaz's arms, and continued, "I tell them every day, just ask them yourself, sir."

The boys stood with an amazingly unembarrassed impassivity at their father's spectacle.

"C'mon Khondoker, enough already," said Shahbaz, finally using his free arm to disengage Khondoker's second hand, and pulling his hand out of the snare. "Now is not the time for all this. I'm happy to see you, and especially your boys. Please, go, just enjoy the party."

"Yes, sir, that's what we're here for," said Khondoker, dipping down unexpectedly to touch Shahbaz's feet.

"What are you doing, Khondoker?! What's come over you today?"

"Sorry, sir, I'm just suddenly so emotional," said Khondoker, straightening up again. "You are turning sixty, and you are so well. Madam and the children so well. It's such a happy day. A big day. It's a big day for me too, sir. You'd be happy to know. Just today we got permission to take my new tower to 55 floors. It'll be done by December–the tallest tower in Dhaka."

Khondoker stood erect, shoulders almost straight. Face beaming and his narrow eyes glittering in their caves. Yellow teeth exposed in their full array. So, that's why you are here! That's what all this show was about. It was a hit, planned and executed. It was nothing short of masterful. He ambushed Shahbaz at the entrance, not because he didn't know better, but because he didn't want to leave the imparting of his news to a chance cue in a conversation. He had come specifically to deliver the news. Job done, he would now leave, before the food was served.

"That's good news indeed, Khondoker," said Shahbaz. "That's very good news. I'm so proud of you. I wish you luck."

He knew not to show emotion at a moment like this. One needed to know how to absorb a good hit without losing composure.

"I knew you would, sir," said Khondoker, still beaming.

"I just hope no one comes up with anything taller anytime soon," said Shahbaz, unable to resist a mild threat.

"They might, sir, but even the World Trade Center, the Petronas Towers, they lost their status. We enjoy our glory as long as it lasts."

"Yes, we do, Khondoker. That's the best we can do," said Shahbaz, moving away from his victorious nemesis to attend to a sudden swell of late arrivals, too many to dump on Belkis alone.

By the time dinner was served, the band had moved on to a Billy Joel number. The singer had turned up late, codeine-loaded, and delivered the classics with aplomb, despite his condition. Shahbaz walked around talking to guests almost in a daze. Familiar faces looked utterly alien. The repeated felicitations rang hollow.

The flashing lights gave him a headache; Shahbaz needed to sit down.

What a day it was! What a day! The party, which, like the birthday, had failed to excite him into the desired mood, lost what little luster it retained after the encounter with Khondoker. Shahbaz scanned the tent an hour later, when most guests were seated at their tables but could not spot Khondoker anywhere. Job done, the assassin had left with his lackeys.

"Are you okay, Baba?" It was Sonya, standing over him with evident concern.

Shahbaz was sitting with his elbows lodged on his thighs, and his face resting heavily in his enjoined palms. He didn't know when he had assumed this pensive and defeated position, that too in public, or how long he had been sitting like that.

"You are sweating, Baba" said Sonya. "What's wrong? Do you want to go inside?"

"No, I'm fine. I just needed to sit down. Get me some water."

Though he had found a secluded corner by the stage, a few of the guests, shunted to the outer rows, had noticed Shahbaz by now. Shahbaz was in no mood to explain to these nincompoops the complications of his life. Or how his sixtieth birthday had passed. Why the things that bothered him mattered. No, he had taken enough shit for one day. Khondoker had taken him by surprise. Shahbaz had to give his protégé credit for lessons well learned.

To eschew the curious onlookers, Shahbaz stood up and grabbed his coat, which had fallen off the chair back.

Sonya came back a few minutes later with a glass of water, and a cold, wet towel. "Baba, it's time to cut the cake," she said.

It's time for a lot more, my girl. It's time for me to make some big moves again. What would be the value of his brand if some upstart could claim to own the tallest tower? What satisfaction in being the largest, if all he could point to were scattered edifices, no matter how numerous? Shahbaz could barely stand to be in this party anymore; he wanted to go into his office–he wanted to think through the options.

A corner of the bandstand had been cleared for the cake-cutting. A police siren outside announced the arrival at the gate of a very late VIP. A string of lights went out without any noise along the right edge of the tent.

Belkis stood behind a table with a giant blue cake in the shape of a guitar–the one detail where Shahbaz had allowed Imtiaz to prevail. The significance of the design evaded him, both at the time of the decision, and certainly now. Where was the boy?

Sonya led him towards the stage. The guitarist lightly thrummed "For He's a Jolly Good Fellow." Guests, mostly done with dinner, gravitated slowly towards the stage with the slow coagulant movement of a giant jellyfish.

Sonya walked one step ahead of Shahbaz. Imtiaz had joined his mother on the stage. A jostle in the other end of the jellyfish suggested that the organism was trying to split to make room for a spearing new species. Wait to see who it is? Or go up to cut the cake first?

As Shahbaz hesitated for a second with one foot on the first step of the stage, a waiter came up beside him, "Sir, if I may–"

What did the waiter want? The blinking lights were driving him mad. They made it harder for him to recognize people. Shahbaz turned, and the face that stared at him threw him into a deep disorientation. He knew the waiter from somewhere, but why should he know a hired waiter?

The synapses fired furiously, but failing to make any connection between the accosting face and known images, deepened his aggravation.

"Sir, you met me this morning–," said the boy helpfully.

You? That candidate? Now, here? Shahbaz was completely beside himself with confusion. How did he get in?

"Sir, I've been meaning to come up to you all evening–"

How did you even get here? Who let you in? Did you pretend to be a waiter? How dare you? All day long I take abuse from everyone, family, rivals, ministers, traffic, laborers–

"Sir, if I may, you really did not...I mean it really wasn't fair–"

That word jolted Shahbaz like an electric shock, the kind torturers administer in dilapidated warehouses with thin wires. And what happened next happened too quickly for anyone to control. Shahbaz planted himself firmly on the steps, as he turned towards the boy, raising his right arm to a full arc. He never quite got to know if the Minister, who, led by Neela, was coming down the aisle, saw the slap. But it landed so hard, the boy fell down into a momentary coma, as the jellyfish emitted a collective gasp, stilled for a second, and then tore off into a confusion of pieces.

Long after the party was over, long after the decorators cleared out all the service and the cutleries, the cloths and the covers, but leaving the canopy and the stage and the lights and baubles that lit up the occasion, Shahbaz was still awake. The party ended sooner than expected.

Belkis sat with Shahbaz for a while and tried to buttress him with assurances about the Minister and repeated the need to take the overdue vacation.

Shahbaz was lost in despair and hostilities so deep and private that no word could penetrate that realm. In fact, another hour with Shahbaz in this state of anguish, and Belkis too would be pulled irretrievably into an abyss, and that too she was willing to suffer, if she could only help him. But, Shahbaz did not allow anyone to help him. He created his own hell, and he alone knew how to clamber out of it. Around two in the morning, Belkis too went to bed, and Shahbaz sat on the verandah. Someone should have turned off the bloody lights!

What a day! What a day! What a day! And soon Imtiaz would be gone again. How he'd miss the boy. For all the frustration Imtiaz caused him, just the sight of him, his animated discourse on his myriad obsessions, was a pure source of joy for Shahbaz. And Sonya! There was a faint but new ray of hope there–she spent more than enough time at work, and she was actually starting to hook new clients. A step ahead of her brother, as she should be as the older sibling, but, to be honest, still far from being ready to receive the full reigns of his empire.

Empire! Even Shahbaz wasn't vain enough to think of his enterprise in such grandiose terms. Though sycophants, even well-wishers, hurled that term at him, when enquiring about its health, especially its future. Enemies used the term to mock him. It didn't matter what you called it–empire, inheritance, legacy–it was what everyone worried about. Emperors, statesmen, tycoons, even little shop owners, they all had the same worry: Who would mind the world when they were gone?

Doctors and lawyers anguished over their children if their heirs did not train to continue their practice. Why mock him alone or his empire or his worries? Professors mused if their protégés would enrich the ideas spawned by them. If not a grand theory, then couldn't some little nugget of knowledge in their field, or sub-field, come to be named after them? With quiet desperation everyone sought a hook with which to hold themselves to history.

It wasn't what he alone thought about when he turned sixty, when he demolished his own party, or when he sat up at four in the morning, with nothing to keep him company but the incessant flicker of maddening strings of little white electric lights in his garden. I must remember never to use these stupid lights again!

He knew tomorrow was another day, and the thoughts that swept him now would provide little solace or guidance to his day-self, ready yet again for battles. But what he knew now was all that he needed to know in that night hour.

People far greater than him had failed to raise a successor or ensure continuity. Marcus Aurelius, the greatest of philosopher-kings, settled for an unremarkable dud like Commodus as his successor. Unable to face the final Manchu assault, led by a peasant soldier, the last Ming Emperor hanged himself from a tree outside the Forbidden City. Shahbaz was captivated even more by the fate of the little known, the forgotten. Palaces reduced to dunes. Poompuhar washed away by a tsunami. Sijilmasa sacked by successive waves of raiders, until not even a pillar was left. Helike lost to an earthquake. Pompeii to volcanic lava. Ubar cratered into an underground water cavern.

But imagine the labor that must have gone into building those cities vanished without a trace! Shahbaz went back into the room and was pleased to see Belkis peacefully asleep. He felt bad that he did not allow her to console him earlier, but was happy to see her at rest now.

Shahbaz retrieved the book on Ubar he had started a few weeks back and came back to the verandah. He found a strange comfort in the example of these lost cities. Nothing lasts; not just in this land of mud and rain, but anywhere. Not in the deserts, nor in the mountains. Cities built of stone and iron disappeared. Still men built new cities, new empires. New lands and new hutments. What men built, its worthiness could not be dismissed because structures collapsed and even the legends, once whole and celebrated, fell to fragments. But, even nothingness survived. Here in his hands was the tale of Ubar, as traceless and forgotten as cities could get, but speaking to him across millennia. He read till dawn broke across the Dhaka sky, and this lost tale fastened Shahbaz, and his solitary, sinking efforts, to a composition of measureless human will.

About the Author

K. Anis Ahmed is a Bangladeshi writer based in Dhaka. He is also an entrepreneur who has founded a liberal arts university, a daily newspaper, and Bangladesh's first certified organic tea garden. He is co-founder of *Bengal Lights*, Bangladesh's most prominent English literary journal. *Good Night, Mr. Kissinger* is his first collection of short stories.